LJ BURKHART

A Demon in the Dawn

A Realm of Queridian Novella

Contents

Prophecy

A line long thought gone
The victim of a con.
Her path will bring the change
For which the realm is rearranged.
The Demon in the Dawn
Will turn into a pawn.
The betrayal that is her unmaking
Will be the realm's breaking.
The Queen of Demons
Will take vengeance for the treason.
Beware.

Chapter 1

Demonica

I brush my ebony hair back, navigating the strands around my black horns. My red eyes peer back at me in my reflection. I have bags under them from the little sleep I've been getting lately. Not only have I been working more than usual, but I've been having nightmares. I never remember exactly what happens in the dreams, but there's always an air of doom to them, like my whole world is going to fall apart. Not that there's anything special about my life. On the contrary, my life is thoroughly boring.

My parents died when I was young. I don't remember anything about them, and I don't have any siblings. I was raised in a brothel since that's where my mother worked as one of the conduits. When she died, the women there raised me. None of them really liked me, but they tolerated me, knowing that as soon as I was old enough, I could help with their duties, mainly in the kitchen and cleaning the establishment.

After all this time, I'm still here. I hate the work, but honestly, there's not much else for a demon to do in Queridian. I've often had the urge to leave my territory. The water calls to me, and

I've always wanted to see the mermaid city and the underwater palace. Not that I would be allowed to go there. I'm just a nobody. Just a demon. The other species in the realm hate us. The only reason they pay any attention to us at all is when they need us to breed with them for specific power traits. It disgusts me. We could offer so much more, *be* so much more than the second-rate citizens the realm considers us.

When I'm ready for work, I head down to the kitchens. That's usually where the madam needs me the most, although she also has me clean the rooms after the clients. That's my *favorite.* Do I need to work on my sarcasm? Probably.

"You're late, Demonica," Kirena comments dryly as I enter.

"I'm having a bad hair day," I retort. She hates my attitude, so I always make sure to lay it on thick just for her.

She rolls her eyes at me. "Take those trays to rooms four and seven." She points to the food that is ready to go with her knife.

I huff as I pick them up and start my shift. I drop off the food to room four first since it's closer. They politely accept the tray and then I'm off to room seven. This one doesn't go nearly as smoothly. I would like to say this rarely happens, but unfortunately, working at a brothel has its disadvantages.

"Well, aren't you a looker? Much prettier than the woman who serviced me. Can I eat this meal off of *you* instead?"

I almost throw up in my mouth, but I'm so used to this happening that I just paste a sweet smile on my face and brush him off. "That's not what I do here, but enjoy your food." I shove the tray in his hands and take off before he can say anything else.

When I'm around the corner, I finally let my shiver free, barely containing my *bleh* of disgust in case he's still able to hear me. I make my way back to the kitchens, and my night continues in much the same way.

My shift finally ends and I plop down on my bed, exhausted after the day's events. I pull out a romance book that I have hidden under my mattress. It's worn after years of me reading and rereading it. I read until my eyes grow tired and I'm drifting off to sleep.

A dream comes to me then. I'm in Mermacovia, swimming up to the underwater palace, but instead of the typical fins, I have tentacles. Even in my sleep-induced state, I'm shocked. The only mermaids who have tentacles are Surseiha's line. Surseiha was the most powerful mermaid queen to ever live. She was called the sea witch, even though she didn't have any witch blood. She often experimented with blood magic and invented new spells and potions.

I'm a demon. There's no way I could be her descendant, but when I wake, I can't get the dream out of my head, and the feeling that it means something important. I'm off at work all day, only half focusing on my job. Kirena notices and lays into me about it. I can't say I care enough to put in more effort.

When my day is finished, I head to my room and take out a dingy old map I have of the realm. I've always wanted to travel to a different territory, but never had the opportunity or the reason. Now I do, even though it may not be real or legitimate. Honestly, it's probably just an excuse to get out of here. I don't care. I'm taking it.

I pack a bag, bringing all my important stuff with me. They will most likely just toss everything that I leave behind. Not that I have much to pack, but I take what I can. When I have everything I need and I'm sure everyone is asleep, I sneak out as quietly as I can. I make a pit stop by the kitchens and stuff my bag full of everything else I can fit. I don't plan on coming back.

Luckily, working at a brothel, everyone sleeps while the sun is up and is awake all night, so I'm able to start my traveling during the day. I head east toward Mermacovia and take a deep breath as I start off on a new adventure.

Chapter 2

Days later, I cross into Mermacovia. I breathe in the salty sea air, and excitement bubbles in my stomach at finally being able to see the ocean. The closer I get, the more motivated I become and I quicken my pace.

When I'm thoroughly worn out, I take a break for lunch. I enjoy the scenery around me as I settle in, dipping my feet in a stream to reduce the inflammation from walking so much. Why couldn't I have been born a mermaid? This is much more glamorous than where I come from, and I'm not even in the city yet.

I pass multiple people on the way, and without fail, they all take one look at the horns on top of my head and a sneer crosses their faces. I sigh, wishing it didn't have to be like this. Demons have always been looked at as less than others, partially because they fear our abilities. We essentially have the power to suck out others' essence, but most of us don't cross that line. It's sacred, and the only ones who have the desire to do it aren't right in the head. My demon rears her head at the snide looks, and I have the urge to snap at them, but I tamp it down.

I continue on my journey to the ocean. The humidity soaks into my skin and I bask in it. I've never felt anything like this before, and despite the treatment from the mermaids, the location more than makes up for it.

It takes me another few hours to reach the coast, and when I get my first glimpse of the sea, tears build behind my eyes. I'm overwhelmed by the enormity of the connection that's mirrored in my being by the water before me. It feels as though a piece of me that was missing my entire life has finally clicked into place.

I can see Allure Isle off in the distance, and I wish for the hundredth time that I could visit the underwater palace. I've heard it's the most beautiful sight in all of Queridian.

I rush forward, running into the ocean and laughing as the water laps over my feet. The salty air sticks to my skin, and I realize how dirty I am. My hair is plastered to my neck from the humidity and my sweat, not to mention the dirt coating my skin from my journey. I'm tempted to strip off my clothing. I am in Mermacovia after all—they don't give a shit about nudity—but I don't feel like taking the time to disrobe. I drop my bag on the beach, wade farther into the water, and dive in headfirst. I'm fully submerged, and it's glorious. The water is the perfect temperature, and the sun beats down on me through the waves.

I may not have grown up by an ocean, but I do know how to swim. Even though there isn't much water in my territory, we did have a lake close by. It was always my escape, and I went at every opportunity. This moment reminds me a bit of that, but even better with the movement of the water and the open space all around me. A strange sensation ripples through my arms, and I almost inhale a lungful of salt water as glowing runes spring to life across them.

I shoot up out of the water, and I'm shocked to see that the runes that decorate my body are casting a glow on the water, lighting it up around me. Someone exclaims behind me, startling me even more. I turn around and meet the eyes of a woman my age. She has aqua-blue hair and sparkling silver eyes, which are currently wide with shock.

"Your Highness! I mean, Your Majesty..." She trails off, and my brow knits in confusion at her words. Majesty? I'm not royal.

She sinks into an awkward bow. It makes me uncomfortable, and regret flares through me that I'm not the royal she thinks I am.

"You've made a mistake. I'm not the queen. Or the princess. Or whoever you think I am."

"Oh, but you are," she says, awe filling her voice as wonder lights her eyes. "Don't you understand? Those markings on your skin—they identify you as Surseiha's descendant. You're the rightful Queen of Queridian," she whispers reverently. I barely hear her over the waves.

When the words sink in, I almost fall back into the water, my legs weak beneath me.

"We need to take you to see the queen immediately. Yemonja will want to know about this." She grabs my hand and starts dragging me into the water. It's then that I realize what she intends.

"Wait! I'm not like you. I can't shift. I'm a demon, not a mermaid."

She finally looks at me properly then, her eyes leaving the marks on my arms and dragging up to my face and horns. She frowns, but nods all the same.

"Demon or not, you're still our queen, and I will make sure you get there safely."

I breathe a little sigh of relief. "What's your name?" I ask.

"Isla."

"Nice to meet you. I'm Demonica."

"The pleasure is all mine, Majesty. Now, I can bring you with me underwater and give you air. Are you comfortable with that?"

I don't know if this is a good idea. I just met this woman. I don't know if I can trust her with something like this, but I guess I could always just break away from her and come up to the surface if I need to. I can hold my breath for longer than most people.

"Can you show me first?"

She nods, grabbing my hand and pulling me farther into the water. When it's deep enough, we plunge below the waves and she pulls me down a little more. I watch in fascination as she shifts. I've never seen it before, and the process is intriguing. A split second later, she's in her mermaid form, her white and blue tail gleaming. Then, she presses her mouth to mine. I'm not expecting it, even though I don't know why this didn't occur to me. Her lips part against mine, but it's not a kiss. Not in the traditional sense. There's no sexuality or romance behind it. I part my own, and in the next second, I feel her breathing air into my lungs.

We pop up from the water a moment later. "So?" she asks.

"Yes. I'm willing to come with you. How do we make this work?"

"Just hang on to me and squeeze my hand when you need a breath. Ready?"

I nod. I don't really feel ready, but I don't think I have much choice right now.

We dive back under, and start swimming. Well, I should say *she* starts swimming. I just hang on for dear life, because we're shooting through the water. I squeeze her hand before I technically need to. I want to make sure that she's going to do what she said before it's too late.

We stop and she gives me a breath immediately, and then

we're off again. I'm relieved that she's keeping her word and I don't have to figure out how to escape up to the surface. Now that I know I can trust her—for this, at least—I look around, admiring my surroundings. At first there's not much to see, but soon a city comes into view. I'm struck by the beauty and enormity of it. I'm actually going to be able to see the underwater palace! I don't know if I'll be able to go inside, but at least I'll see the outside.

The closer we get to the city, the more crowded it becomes. Everyone we pass gives us confused looks until they spot the glowing runes on my skin. Then they look at me with respect and deference, bowing their heads to me as we pass. This is so strange. I never could have imagined something like this happening to me.

We round a corner, and it's then that I see the underwater palace. It takes everything in me not to gasp at the sight. I do not want to inhale a lungful of salt water right now. It's magnificent. The building plunges out of the seafloor and the bottom half is mostly all windowed and open. There are multiple mermaids swimming around in it, and from here it almost looks like a display. Above it sits the actual castle. It's lit from within and underneath with glowing blue and yellow lights, illuminating the rest of the water around it. Turrets jut up everywhere, and the top half of the castle is actually above the surface. I bet it's so there can be a section for those who can't function underwater.

We swim up to the main gates and are let through after a few moments. I can't be sure, but it seems as though Isla is communicating with them. I know some things about other species, but demons aren't told much, so I wasn't aware this was possible.

We enter and are taken to Yemonja in the center of the palace.

I'm amazed at the structure of the building and the materials they use. From what I can tell, the mermaids have used coral and seaweed for a few reasons. One, it makes it look more natural and beautiful. Two, it's already a part of the underwater landscape and therefore won't break down easily. Three, it can be used defensively if need be, not only to hide behind, but also as a weapon. It makes sense to me, but it's still so different from what I'm used to seeing that it catches me by surprise.

We finally reach Yemonja. She's sitting on a throne made of coral and seashells, and I initially think there's no way that can be comfortable, but then I spot a clear squishy substance separating her body from the throne. It might be jellyfish tops, and the thought makes me shudder.

Yemonja herself is gorgeous in the classic mermaid fashion. She has peach-colored hair that cascades past her waist. The top is braided intricately, but the bottom is loose and flowing. A huge crown of seashells, fish bones, and pearls sits on her head.

When she sees me, her orange eyes widen. She looks at Isla and I observe her as her facial expressions change. It's clear they're communicating somehow, and I wish I could hear what was being said. She gestures up with her finger before taking off without seeing if we follow.

Isla gives me a breath before we make our way up, up, up. We eventually reach a set of stairs and Isla releases me so I can walk up on my own to the surface and the upper portion of the castle.

Yemonja is striding ahead, naked and uncaring. This portion of the palace doesn't seem to be nearly as populated, and I'm assuming most mermaids prefer to be underwater. She heads into a room and I follow quickly behind her, my clothes soaking the floor where I walk, but I don't have anything to dry myself with. Isla is right behind me, and when we enter the room,

Yemonja is already in a robe on another throne.

"Speak," she orders me.

My brows fly up. If I thought she would be nicer to me like Isla, I'm sorely mistaken. "What do you want me to say?"

She narrows her eyes at me. "What kind of trick is this?"

"I don't know what you mean. Honestly. I'm a demon. I left my territory because I had a dream that I was here and was swimming around with tentacles. I felt compelled to come, and when I entered the ocean, these markings showed up on my skin. I had no idea what they meant until Isla told me."

She looks me over thoroughly. By now my markings have faded, but the memory of them is burned into my mind.

"Well, if what you say is true, it seems you are the rightful queen."

"That's what Isla said, and honestly, I am not ready for that. And how do you know this isn't some kind of trick like you said?"

"Those marks cannot be mimicked by anyone. Believe me, others have tried and failed, but their marks were missing something fundamental that yours aren't. Surseiha imbued her bloodline with a special kind of blood magic. No one knows exactly what or how she did it, but that's how those marks appear on your skin. I can *feel* Surseiha's power in them. It calls to all mermaids, and that's what those other imposters were missing. Her magic and our ability to sense it."

"Then why did you ask me if it was a trick?"

"I had to make sure. You have to admit that it's suspicious for you to just show up out of nowhere after all these years. And I must reluctantly admit that I was in denial at first."

I nod. I can imagine that she's not happy about having to give up her crown. To a demon of all people.

"It is our law that anyone from Surseiha's line rule. You do not have a choice to be ready or not." She stands and steps in front of me, taking her crown off. "You will lead our people, Your Majesty," she says, placing it on my head before sinking down to her knees in front of me.

Chapter 3

Her words don't sink in. Neither does the fact that she's kneeling in front of me while her crown sits on my head. I reach up to touch the rough circlet, and when my fingers connect with it, a zing runs through me. The marks on my body start glowing again, and everything finally clicks in my head. Fuck. I'm the new queen. I have instant regret for my decision to leave home.

There's a mirror on the wall across from me and I meet my own gaze. The crown fits perfectly around my horns, and my body glows a soft blue. I'm able to see every place on my body where the runes run now, and I have to admit they're beautiful. I truly look like a queen.

I gaze down at Yemonja and find an expression on her face I can't quite decipher. A mixture of sadness and joy mingle together on her features. I can understand that she's upset at the loss of her position. I am taking her crown after all, but the joy catches me off guard.

"Why are you happy?" I ask.

"Because we've been waiting for Surseiha's heir to rule for so long. We'd lost hope you would show up."

"So, what now?"

"Can I stand, Your Majesty?" Yemonja asks.

My eyes widen. "You don't have to ask me."

"Actually I do. Keep that in mind. Anyone who bows before you needs permission to rise." There's an amused look on her face.

"Oh. Of course. Please stand."

She does and then she answers my original question. "Technically you aren't queen yet. You will need to have a coronation, at which point you will be in charge of the whole of Queridian. Until that time, I need to train you on how to be a ruler and educate you on everything happening in the realm."

"That sounds sensible. Where will I stay?"

"Here, of course. You'll be in the upper portion of the castle since you aren't able to shift into your mermaid form. Also, for the time being, I think it would be unwise to travel to the islands. This is all so new, and there are bound to be differing opinions on the matter. Until you are formally trained and we have a date set for your coronation, I think you will be safest here where I can offer you my protection."

I nod. That makes sense. I might hate it eventually, but right now I can handle that. I've wanted to be in this exact place for longer than I can remember after all.

"I'll have the servants move my possessions out of the royal chamber to make room for you. Where are your belongings?"

"I didn't bring much with me, but I left my bag on the beach."

She nods. "I'll also contact the seamstress to have some clothing made for you. You're royal and you need to look it. I'll also have an assortment of things you'll need for your bed chamber brought to you and you can take your pick."

All of this feels extremely overwhelming, and I almost have a moment where I tell her she doesn't need to do all of that, but that's not how a queen would conduct herself. So instead, I hold my head high and nod.

"Thank you."

She smiles approvingly. She was most likely expecting me to deny her assistance. "You're welcome, Your Majesty."

I feel just as uncomfortable with her addressing me as such, but figure I'll have to get used to it soon enough.

"For now, I'll have someone draw you a bath and get you cleaned up. You need a lot of work, and I'm sure you're exhausted from your travels."

I bristle at the "You need a lot of work" comment, but before I can respond, she's striding off, Isla following. I'm left alone with my thoughts, and I begin pacing. I'm reeling, and I have no idea how to handle all of these changes and process this new information.

I'm just starting to think that maybe I should take off, my anxious energy getting the better of me, when a servant walks in, bowing. "Your Majesty, I'm Riva. I'll be one of your lady's maids. I have a bath drawn for you, if you'll follow me?"

I have a lady's maid. Actually, more than one. The thought is somehow more jarring than anything yet. I've *always* taken care of myself. Or least since I was old enough to, which was probably when I was five or so.

"Your Majesty?"

I shake myself out of my stupor and follow her without a word. The castle is beautiful, but this section doesn't seem lived in much. Or at least there's not many people occupying it at the moment, likely because the sun is still up. I'm glad that I became accustomed to being awake during the day as opposed to the night while traveling, otherwise I'd have one more thing to adjust to.

I'm led to a room larger than any I've ever seen before. I'm gaping at it in wonder when Riva speaks. "This isn't the royal quarters. They're removing all of Que—I mean Yemonja's belongings. She thought this room would do for now until they have it ready for you."

My eyes almost bug out of my head. "The royal quarters are *bigger* than this?"

She chuckles. "Yes, my queen. By quite a lot. You'll have multiple rooms. This is simply one of the guest quarters."

Gods. I don't know how my life changed so drastically in a single afternoon.

Riva leads me to the bathroom, and I gasp. It's even more magnificent than the bedroom. The tub is big enough to swim in, and it's filled with sweet-smelling bubbles of all different colors. I almost squeal in delight, but refrain when I remember Riva is still here. There's another woman standing in the corner, looking like she's trying to melt into the wall.

"Who are you?" I ask.

"Miranda, my queen," she says quietly.

"She's another lady's maid, Your Majesty," Riva adds helpfully.

"Oh, of course. Nice to meet you both."

They give me strange looks before looking down again.

"Are you going to stand here, or can I get into the bath?"

"We're to bathe you, my queen."

I almost scoff, but refrain. "I'm perfectly capable of washing myself. I've been managing it my entire life."

"With all due respect, Your Majesty, you aren't aware of how mermaids bathe. Yemonja instructed us to make you presentable."

I bristle at the insinuation that I'm not well groomed, but as I look at myself in the mirror, I think she might have a point. My hair is brittle and dull looking, my skin is a bit patchy from all the travel and sun exposure, and my nails are jagged. On top of all that, I can imagine that I don't smell the best. The swim probably helped, but I'm looking forward to washing myself with actual soap.

I nod my consent before undressing and sinking down into the heavenly water. I let out a soft sigh before dipping my hair underwater, ready for them to begin.

When I resurface, Riva and Miranda move in. Riva tends to my hair, lathering it up with a wash that smells like something sweet and sultry. I moan as her fingers dig into my scalp, massaging away the tension from my trip and the stress of the day.

Miranda starts on my toes, lifting them out of the water and clipping my toenails and filing them. It's both wonderful and strange to have others do these tasks for me, but I better get used to it.

I rinse my hair out per Riva's instructions before she puts some sort of oil on my ends, twisting the strands into a bun so it can soak in. Miranda then has me stand, and the two ladies rub my entire body down with a salt scrub, exfoliating off all the dead skin, they tell me.

I rinse the scrub from my body and the oil from my hair, and then they're ushering me out of the tub. Riva twists my hair into a lovely braid as Miranda clips and files my fingernails and then paints them and my toes.

The last thing to do is dress and do my makeup. Riva takes care of my face while Miranda picks out an outfit for me. She assures me they'll have a wardrobe made for me soon, but these will do in the meantime.

Hours later, I'm ready. I look in the mirror and don't even recognize myself. My face is immaculate, my hair is gleaming, and my nails shimmer in the soft light. I gasp at my reflection when Riva puts my crown back on my head. None of this feels real. I'm positive that at any moment I'm going to wake at the brothel, this all being a torturously beautiful dream.

"The qu—I mean Yemonja would like to have dinner with you, my queen," Riva tells me. I don't miss the fact that she keeps almost calling her Queen Yemonja, and I'm sure that there will be an adjustment period for everyone involved.

I nod. "I'm ready."

She escorts me to the dining hall, and there are so many mouth-watering scents that my stomach growls loudly. I didn't realize how hungry I was, but I haven't been able to eat much on the road.

Yemonja is sitting at the table, the seat to the right of the head. It's clear that chair is meant for the ruler. Me. I gulp nervously as I take my seat. Yemonja smiles politely at me, and I wonder how difficult it was for her not to sit where I am. This was her spot until today.

I take in the amount of food on the table, and I'm floored. I'll have to watch what I eat so I don't gain a ton of weight. Not now though. I reach forward, ready to try some of everything, but Yemonja stops me.

"A queen does not serve herself. The servants will attend to us."

I sigh. This is going to take some getting used to, but I nod all the same. Instead, I take a drink from my wine goblet as the staff loads all the food onto my plate. As soon as they're finished, I pick up my fork and she stops me again.

"That fork is not for that dish. You want to use this one instead." She picks up the outermost utensil.

I almost growl in frustration. I'm so hungry and tired. I don't feel like going through queen lessons right now. "Can I just eat?" I snap at her.

Her brows rise in surprise and admonishment. I'm sure she's not used to others talking to her like this and I know she wants to punish me for it. But she's not queen anymore. I am.

"Of course, Your Majesty," she says evenly, though I can see something burn behind her gaze.

I tear into my food. I know I shouldn't be eating like this now that I'm royal, but I don't care. I'm starving. Yemonja watches me distastefully, but I ignore her. I can't pay attention to the perfect way she's sitting and the careful way she's eating. It's all too much right now.

I finish eating before she does, even though I had much more on my plate. She eyes me the entire meal, but I pay her no mind. When she's *finally* done, she speaks.

"There's much I need to teach you."

"Not tonight," I say. I can't right now.

"But we really have a lot to go ove—"

"Yemonja, not tonight. Tomorrow," I say firmly, but not as rudely as I did earlier now that I've eaten.

She nods once, looking increasingly displeased the more I speak. "With your permission then, I'll retire to my quarters." I wonder how much it frustrates her to have to ask me for permission now.

"Of course. I'll meet with you tomorrow."

She bows before leaving, and then I'm alone at the table. I have them pour me one more glass of wine, taking it with me back to my rooms. I'm going to sleep well tonight.

Chapter 4

The next few months pass quickly. The kingdom has been notified that there's been a change in ruler. Or there will be as soon as I have my coronation. Yemonja trains me every single day on many topics.

The first is queenly etiquette. This instruction is the most time-consuming, and the one that needs the most work. Some moments are easy for me and others are more difficult. Yemonja admonishes me on this frequently. A queen needs to be at her best at *all* times. You never know who is going to see you, and you need to be admired by the entire realm. You don't want an uprising. I'm getting better, but it takes constant focus.

The second topic of training is my duties. There's much the ruler of the realm is responsible for, including signing off on things and approving literally *everything*, and occasionally meeting up with the council to discuss the goings-on in each of the territories.

Yemonja tells me that it will still probably be a solid six months to a year before I am ready to fully take over, and the prospect feels grueling and intimidating at the same time. The thought of running the realm on my own makes me want to curl up in bed, but at the same time it's strangely exciting. I never thought I would be in this position in a million years, and look at me now.

I wish I could go back to the brothel and shove it in their faces.

Yemonja mentions throwing a ball to introduce me to the kingdom in two months, and my heart beats excitedly. I've never been to a ball before. I want to wear something gorgeous and have men fawn all over me. That thought causes nerves to flutter in my stomach. I've never been with a man before either, even though I grew up in a brothel. I know what happens, of course, but I've never had the opportunity of a romantic relationship before. Men coming into the brothel aren't exactly looking for a relationship. Not to mention that they're not the greatest of catches.

With the date of the ball set, Yemonja kicks my training up, wanting to make sure that I'm ready to face the kingdom and won't make a fool out of myself. The royal seamstress has already begun creating my dress, and I smile to myself every time I think of putting on a *gown*. That is an opportunity I never thought I would get, but here I am. Having worked with the seamstress before, I can already tell it's going to be extravagant.

A month before the ball, I receive a letter from the son of the grand master for the fae, Theon. I'm somewhat intrigued when he tells me that he will be at the ball and can't wait to meet me. Apparently he's wanted to form a close relationship between the mermaids and the fae for a long time, but Yemonja was never interested in marrying, especially outside of her own species.

I, on the other hand, am already a different species. It would be hard to marry another mermaid with me not being able to shift. I'm sure they would want to spend a lot of time underwater, and that's not something I'm able to do.

I suppose that now I'm going to be in a position of power, I'll have to start thinking about marriage. Especially one that would be advantageous. It wouldn't hurt to have the fae backing me. I also don't want to marry someone if I don't at least enjoy their company. I'm not delusional. I know that love matches for royals are few and far between, but I at least want respect and friendship. If it turns to love eventually, all the better.

I have a few other potential suitors, but Theon's letter warms my heart the most. He's a beautiful writer, and I feel like I already know him just from his words alone. I read it every night before I go to bed. I know that's incredibly naive and innocent, but I can't help it. Finally hearing that someone wants me, and not just for my body, ignites a fire in my blood and causes butterflies to erupt in my stomach.

Yemonja has already discussed marriage with me and warned me that I will need to make the smartest decision for the kingdom and my throne. With the exception of that comment, she hasn't given any sort of hint as to what she thinks I should do, for which I'm grateful. This is a decision I'd like to make on my own.

I decide to write Theon back as well as my other potential suitors. Realistically, I don't really care about any of them apart from Theon, but I know I need to keep my options open; especially if I meet him at the ball and he's not what I'm expecting. I keep the letters to my other admirers generic, telling them I look forward to meeting them at the ball. The letter to Theon, however, includes more detail about my life, and I express my thanks for his words and interest. I emphasize how excited I am to meet him.

In the following weeks, I concentrate hard on my training, really not wanting to embarrass myself now that I have potential spouses to impress. Yemonja notices and remarks on it one day. I assure her that I'm just feeling more motivated to do well by her and the kingdom. She doesn't believe me in the least, but

I'm grateful that she doesn't call me out on it.

I receive another letter a week before the ball, and I'm delighted when I see Theon's beautiful script. I hastily open it and am already swooning. He tells me all about his life and territory, and I get to know him a little bit better. I'm happy that we've already established a base before we meet in person. It will make this whole situation with him less awkward.

I'm excited and nervous at the same time. At first the ball seemed so close, and I didn't feel prepared for it. Now I wish it would just get here already. I'm anxious to meet Theon, and for the kingdom to meet their new queen.

I'm now to the point where I'm able to meet other significant people without embarrassing myself or Yemonja. It's been a long time coming, and so much work, but I'm grateful that it's paying off.

My dress is finished with only six days to spare, and I'm thrilled. Normally I wouldn't care too much, but since I want to look nice for Theon, I'm relieved. I was starting to worry that it wouldn't be ready in time, but I had words with the seamstress a few days ago, making sure she knew how important it was. I may have been a bit harsh, but she needs to understand who I am. Yemonja isn't their queen anymore. I am.

The night before the ball, I'm just finishing my training session, planning to head to bed. I need to get in my beauty sleep for the ball tomorrow, however, a servant finds me first.

"Your Majesty, there is someone here to see you."

I huff irritably. It's been a long day, and the last thing I want is a visitor. "Tell them to leave, Henry."

"I don't think you want me to do that, Your Majesty. And my name is Hubert."

"You dare question your queen, *Henry?*" My words are lined

with the threat.

The servant drops his eyes, bowing his head slightly. "Not at all, Your Majesty. I just didn't think you would want to upset one of the potential suitors."

My ears perk up. "Well, why didn't you tell me that in the first place?"

I rush forward as my heartbeat quickens. I'm not sure who exactly is here, but excitement pulses inside me all the same. I take a moment to compose myself and make sure I look nothing but perfect.

I let the servant open the door for me, and when I step through, I see the most gorgeous man I've ever laid eyes on. Ice-blond hair, cold blue eyes, pointed ears, and full lips sprouting a charming smile. Holy Gods.

"Your Majesty." The handsome stranger bows, his voice like liquid sex. "It's wonderful to finally meet you in person. I hope that you don't mind that I came to visit you early. I simply couldn't wait until tomorrow."

My heartbeat quickens even further. "Theon?"

That smile grows until it lights up his face. "Yes, Your Majesty. It's a pleasure to meet you."

Chapter 5

Theon is here. He's *here.* I don't know what to do with myself. He's gorgeous, and everything I was picturing. Swoony, charming, handsome. Now that he's in my presence, I have no idea what to say to him. I wasn't mentally prepared to meet him *today.* I'm well aware of my appearance—I'm nowhere near as presentable as I had planned for our first meeting.

He stares at me expectantly, and I realize I haven't responded. Or said anything for that matter, except for his name. I fumble for words, my mouth feeling like it's twice its normal size.

"I— You're here earlier than I thought."

His smile is panty-melting. "I thought I would surprise you. And I wanted to see you before your attention was stolen away by the entire realm. This way we can get to know each other without you having the obligation of schmoozing other people of importance," he says earnestly while grasping my hands in his.

I giggle and nod. "That makes sense." Gods. I sound like a naive little virgin. I mean, I technically *am,* but that doesn't justify the behavior in front of the man I'm essentially already in love with who wants to marry me to secure an alliance between our species. I'm rambling in my own head, while outwardly I'm hardly managing a word. Better than the alternative, I acknowledge, and take a deep breath to shake off my anxiety.

He gives me a knowing look and seems to take pity on me, because he doesn't mention the fact that I'm barely speaking. "Would you care to show me around? I've never seen the castle before."

I nod emphatically. "Yes, of course. Are you staying here at the palace?"

"I was hoping to. It would give us more time to get to know each other."

"I would love that. I'll have one of the servants get a room ready for you." I order the servant who notified me that I had a visitor that Theon will be needing a room. When he runs off to do my bidding, I take Theon's offered arm.

I grasp it firmly, marveling at the strong muscles I feel underneath my hand. He sure is a fine specimen. I would be a lucky woman to marry him just based on his looks alone. I wonder what our children would look like. I blush at the thought. We're nowhere near thinking about that yet. Although, since I'm considering marriage prospects, maybe it's not too soon.

Of course, he notices. "What are you thinking about?"

I clear my throat as embarrassment tinges my cheeks an even darker red. "Oh, nothing."

"Oh, it must be something *really* good by the look on your face," he teases, nudging me with his elbow.

"You'll never know."

"Why not?"

"Because then I'd have to kill you, and you're far too pretty for that."

"Oh, so you think I'm pretty, do you?"

My embarrassment just keeps mounting, even when I think it can't get any worse. Instead of responding verbally, I slap him lightly on the chest. He chuckles, the husky sound making something throb between my legs.

He spares me after that and I show him my palace. He seems taken with it, and I rejoice in the fact that he enjoys my castle. My domain. And if we marry, *his* domain as well.

We leisurely stroll through the rooms, wandering together. It took me a while to discover all the secrets this place had to offer, but luckily, I'm able to show him everything I wish without getting lost. The areas that I'm not as familiar with are in the underwater section of the palace. Since I don't have a mermaid form, I haven't been able to explore it hardly at all. I've been down there only a handful of times, and depending upon the assistance of another mermaid is not preferred. I don't want to be seen as reliant.

My subjects are accustomed to having a mermaid queen as the sovereign. One who can be in the water alongside them, and rule below just as she does above. They don't need any reminders of the fact that I'm unable to accomplish that. I think a large number of them still view Yemonja as their queen. I can't have that.

I've been brooding on this lately, but now with a strong potential fae suitor on my arm, I make a conscious decision to crack the whip, so to speak. I want them to both respect me and *fear* me, achieving the balance that defines a great leader.

At the end of the tour, I show Theon where my quarters are located. He eyes them as if he wants to ask if he can come inside, but refrains. The servant, the one who's name I can never remember—Horace, maybe—takes that moment to arrive and tell us that Theon's rooms are ready. I both curse him and thank him in my head.

As much as I already adore Theon, I'm not prepared for that

quite yet. We just met, even though it feels as if I've known him forever through his letters. I'm a virgin, and the fact that I'm now a queen with my virtue intact makes it easier to wait for my wedding night. I mean, I've lasted this long already, right?

He bids me good night, kissing my hand like a perfect gentleman, before following whatever-his-name-is to his quarters. I sag against the doorway, trying to control my emotions. I'm already falling hard for him, but I think it would be wise to keep my options open with my other potential suitors.

I go to bed, equally exhausted and exhilarated. The events of the past few weeks leave me both excited and anxious for the ball tomorrow. Then the fact that Theon showed up early...it's all too much for my nerves to take. I lie in bed, awake, for longer than I would like. I sleep restlessly that night.

The next morning, I wake up early, not able to contain my nerves and excitement for one more moment. I want to see Theon again. I want to get ready and put on my extravagant gown for the ball. I want to dance the night away and never come back down from the high I know I'll experience.

I make myself as beautiful as possible for the day. The ball isn't until that night, so I don't have to start preparing until this afternoon, but I'm hoping to see Theon before then, and I want to look my best, since I didn't have the opportunity the night before.

When I feel satisfied, I make my way to breakfast, ensuring my servants extend an invitation for Theon to join me. He shows up shortly after, and the fact that I'm able to meet his gaze without blushing is an improvement. I inwardly congratulate myself on the small victory.

"Your Majesty, thank you for inviting me to join you for breakfast."

"Thank you for accepting."

We start eating, and all I can think about are all of the lessons Yemonja drilled into me about eating in front of others. As a result, I'm fairly certain I look stiff and uncomfortable for the duration of the meal.

I'm still extremely shy and have no idea what to talk to him about. For some reason, it's much easier to converse through letters and not face-to-face. Theon is patient with me, though, and takes the reins.

He asks about my upbringing. Most people have heard the basics, that I'm a demon, and didn't know about my heritage until I arrived here. But hardly anyone knows that I was raised in a brothel. I want to keep that secret from my subjects, but I decide to share it with Theon. There's a good chance he will be my husband, and as such, it's information he should have.

"I'd wager that was a difficult upbringing," he remarks.

I melt, relieved that he's not uncomfortable about it. "It was, but I never had to do any sex work."

"Were you a servant there?"

I nod. I'm blushing. I despise this part of my past. I look down, ashamed and unable to meet his eyes. I'm a queen now (or will be as soon as I have my coronation), but it feels as though the servant girl at the brothel was a completely different person. I wish that I could cut out that part of my history.

Theon grabs my hand. "It doesn't matter, darling. Your past is just that. You're a queen now, and everyone will soon see how marvelous you are."

If I wasn't already a puddle at his feet, that statement would've done it. I beam at him. He sees me like no one else has in my entire life.

We continue our meal, and the awkwardness eases. He's

settled my nerves, and I wonder if I'll feel this way about any of my other potential suitors. Doubtful.

"I'll see you at the ball, my queen." He kisses my hand as we part ways.

Gods, he's *swoony.* I'm sure my face is the shade of a tomato as I squeak out a reply. "Okay." I mentally berate myself for my lack of eloquence. He probably thinks I'm stupid on top of everything else, but he just gives me a knowing smirk.

I head back to my room, intent on preparing for the rest of the day. I know that I'll be ready in time, but this way I won't be worrying about it.

I summon my servants to work on me. I need to be breath-taking tonight. There's no other alternative. I want all of my suitors to be falling all over themselves to get my attention.

I let the mermaids work their magic, and hours later when I look in the mirror, I'm just as beautiful as I was hoping.

Chapter 6

I don't have a crown yet. Technically Yemonja gave me one when she found out I was Surseiha's descendant, but I'm not able to wear it yet. Not until my coronation. I am also having a different one commissioned. I'm a whole new type of queen, and I want everyone to see it. Until then, I make do with what I have, which is a shit ton of hair, and horns. I have my servants make me my own crown fashioned out of my flowing locks. It's currently a mass of braided intricacy that frames my obsidian horns. They want to add flowers, but that's not my style in the least. I do allow them to add a few shells.

My makeup is applied in a bold fashion, highlighting my eyes and accentuating my lips. My lips are the same shade of red as my irises, my eyeshadow mirrors the darkness of my hair, and a blush and glimmery powder highlights my cheekbones. I scrutinize my face in the mirror and am satisfied with the effect I was hoping to achieve—alluring and ferocious.

The most incredible part of my look, though, is my dress. The torso is tight-fitted and boned like a corset, with a sweetheart neckline. Intricate black lace curves around my shoulders and comes down my chest to swirl above my breasts. Black fabric covers both sides of my upper body with a section of see-through material down the middle of my torso. The dress flows outward slightly from my waist down, growing more detailed as it descends. The see-through section flows into a white-blue color, and has bronze swirls with a smoke-like pattern behind it. Once the fabric reaches the floor, the hem is a sparkly blue. The outer layer is black, embellished with a design that resembles the patterns of tree roots.

Overall, the effect is stunning. I feel more like a queen now than I ever have before. I spritz myself with my most seductive perfume, and I'm as ready as I'll ever be.

The servant—Harry or whatever his name is—tells me the ball is officially underway, and that all of my potential suitors have arrived. Perfect. I make my way down to the ballroom and am announced. The room goes silent as the doors open. Surprisingly, I'm not nervous, and know my appearance and newly found awareness of my position is granting me courage. I am the queen of the realm, even if it's not official yet.

All eyes are glued to me as I meet Yemonja at the throne. I make sure to keep my head held high and not look at anyone. They aren't important. I am. For the first time in my life, I am the most important person in the room.

Yemonja smiles at me approvingly as I approach. I haven't embarrassed her so far, and I don't intend to.

She looks out over the crowd. "I'm sure by now all of you have heard the joyous news. Surseiha's heir has finally presented herself. Our dear Demonica didn't know that she was a descendant until she came to our lovely territory and was born again in our waters. Surseiha's marks appeared on her skin as a sign of her arrival."

Yemonja fails to mention the fact that she rejected that knowledge as soon as she was informed. She didn't accept it until she came to her senses and realized that I couldn't have fabricated the marks.

Yemonja lifts a bowl filled with Mermacovia's waters and holds it between us. "My queen, show them."

I bite back my growl at her order. I'm the queen. No one orders *me*. Especially not in front of my subjects. I harden my eyes at her subtly, unable to do anything else in front of the crowd. I dip my hands into the bowl, and my skin begins glowing with the marks of my ancestor. The onlookers gasp in elated shock.

"Her coronation will be held as soon as she finishes her training. In the meantime, she's open to meeting potential suitors, but does not need a king to rule beside her if she does not wish. For now, she would like us all to rejoice and as she gets to know her subjects!"

The crowd cheers and I grant them a modest smile, though I'm turning into anything *but*. I'm not ready to reveal my ruthlessness. Not yet, anyway.

The party fully commences, and I revel in it. I see Theon eyeing me from the other side of the room, his gaze heating as he takes in my appearance. I ignore him and accept a dance from a random male. I can feel Theon watching me, and I put on a show for him. I want him jealous. I want him to *think* he needs to compete for my attention.

I give the man who I don't give one shit about the same looks I give Theon. He beams at the attention, and I mentally roll my eyes at him. He doesn't hold a candle to Theon. I keep my mind on the strict dance lessons I received, and even though I didn't enjoy them, I'm grateful for them now when I'm able to move gracefully around the dance floor, the center of everyone's observation.

I move from one dance partner to the next. I do meet some attractive men, but none hold my focus. I can't stop thinking about the one man in the room who I want to approach me, but he seems to be letting me socialize.

After what feels like hours, he finally taps on the shoulder of the man I'm dancing with. "May I cut in?"

The man who's name I can't seem to remember for the life of me, nor do I care, sputters something about the song not being over, but neither of us pay him any mind. Theon sweeps me into his arms and expertly spins me around the dance floor. I try not to melt, I really do. I have to play this right, after all, but as soon as his skin touches mine, I'm a goner.

"You look stunning tonight, my queen."

"Thank you," I breathe. "You look incredible too."

He smiles at me and pulls me a little more firmly against him. I suck in a sharp breath as I feel the evidence of his arousal pressing against my belly through the layers of my dress. His eyes heat at the sound.

"Do you know how crazy I was going watching you dance with every fucker in this room except me?"

"Then why didn't you come up to me until now?"

"I was hoping you'd approach me and make fools of them all. But now that you're in my arms, no one will doubt that they have any chance."

I raise my brows at him. "What makes you so sure of that? I've told you nothing of the sort. I could want someone else that I've already danced with."

He chuckles deeply, leaning in close to whisper in my ear. "I don't think so, my little demon. I can see how I affect you. I can *smell* how much you want me. I know none of these other 'men' did that to you. Only me."

My heart beats at his words. He's right, of course, but I don't want him to know that yet. Somehow he turned the game against me, seeing right through me. I don't know what's gotten into him. Yesterday and this morning he was such a gentleman, but tonight he's more *wild*. I can't say I don't enjoy it.

My breaths come faster, even as the dance becomes slower and more intimate. His hand roams a little lower down my back, resting just above my backside. I'm torn between wanting him to move it even lower and shoving his hand farther up. He smiles smugly, as if he knows what I'm thinking.

"Say yes."

"To what?" I ask, a little breathless.

"To being mine. To marrying me. To letting me love you."

I gasp at his words. I've never been loved by anyone. It's what I want more than anything. But there's no way for him to know that.

I search his eyes, looking for any sort of deceit, but find none. I want to believe him so badly. "You don't even know me," I whisper.

"Don't I? We've been writing to each other. I don't *not* know you."

"If I agree to this, I won't marry you right away. I want to get to know you better."

He smiles as if I've already told him yes. "That's fine. If you want, we can marry and have your coronation ceremony together. That way we can both get our crowns at the same time."

My lips quirk upward. I like the sound of that. "I won't be crowned for another six months."

"That's plenty of time to get to know each other, my little demon."

That's the second time he's called me that, and strangely I find myself savoring it. "Okay."

His brows rise. "Okay?"

"Yes. I'll marry you."

His smile lights up the room, making my heart swell, and in the next second, he's pulling me into him, kissing me fully on the mouth. It starts out as something quick and fleeting, but as soon as our lips meet, it swiftly becomes heated.

I've never been properly kissed before, and I feel like I could drown in his kisses. I would die happy, too, I think as his tongue plunders my mouth. I know we shouldn't be doing this in front of the entire court, but I can't bring myself to care. My body is on fire like it's never been before, and I'm extremely tempted to drag him off the dance floor and straight back to my rooms. But I just know that Yemonja would lecture me to the ends of Queridian if I did that. Yemonja. Fuck.

I break away, my face flaming as I look around the room. All eyes are on us, even if some people are attempting to go about their business and be discreet. I meet the former queen's eyes across the room, and she is *fuming*.

I hold my chin high and glare back at her. This is *my* decision. *I* am the queen now. Not her. She seems to understand, and she relents, nodding slightly, but I know this isn't over. She will be having a conversation with me about this tomorrow.

The song ends, and I break away from Theon to take a seat, my feet and back aching from dancing for so long. I have Hugo bring me food and wine, needing some fuel to get through the rest of the party.

Theon sticks close to me for the duration of the evening. I can't help but appreciate the possessiveness. Every time a male looks in my direction, he basically snarls at him. I take notice of the huge difference from the beginning of the night when he was letting everyone and their father dance with me without seeming to have a care in the world. I guess he doesn't want any other man to think they have a chance with me now that I've told him I'll marry him.

I resist the urge to shovel food into my mouth, thinking heavily on Yemonja's lessons. I take my time, sitting properly and using the correct utensils. She nods at me approvingly, and I try to tamp down on the rush of pride, but it's difficult. Not that I don't think I should be proud; I've come a long way from the servant girl from the brothel who traipsed into Mermacovia. However, I don't want the emotion to be in relation to *her*. I refuse to seek permission or approval from *anyone*, especially the former queen. I relish the thought of that word—*former*. I can do things on my own now that I am the true queen.

The rest of the night passes quickly, and I revel in the attention that I receive from everyone in attendance. I've never experienced anything like this before. I've always been the invisible one. No longer.

"Are you going to announce our engagement, my queen?" Theon asks from beside me, putting a possessive hand on my knee. The heat of his palm sends a thrill through me.

"Not yet. They have a fairly good idea about your intentions after your kiss earlier," I scold him. I don't want him thinking that he's in control of anything. This is *my* decision, and he doesn't need to think that he can do whatever he wants with no consequences.

He nods, subdued for now after my reprimand. I have a feeling that I'm going to need to keep him in line, and in return he's going to keep me on my toes.

When I've had my fill of dramatics for the evening, watching my subjects get more and more inebriated, I turn in for the night.

Theon escorts me to my rooms. "Can I kiss you again, my

queen? Now that we're alone?"

I narrow my eyes at him, but a slight smile grazes my mouth and a blush rises to my cheeks, giving away that I'm not nearly as unaffected as I would have him believe.

"You may."

He inches closer, his mouth hovering just above mine. I bring my face up, willing him to close the distance, but he waits there, building the anticipation. I lick my lips, hoping that will do the trick, and I'm rewarded with his eyes blazing with arousal as they lock on the motion. His mouth is on mine in the next moment, and I moan into it. It's even better than the kiss at the ball because there's no one here to see. I know that this is just for us. That he isn't putting on a show or staking a claim in front of the entire realm.

His tongue darts out and travels along the seam of my lips and I open for him, my own tongue reaching out to meet his. His arms wrap around my waist as he pulls me firmly against him. I can feel his impressive length pressing into my belly, and a shudder works its way through me as I imagine what he can do with it.

He breaks away just the slightest to whisper against my lips, "Let me follow you inside, my little demon." It's a statement, not a question, his ego showing itself even more evidently now. He doesn't think I'll turn him away.

I want to say yes. I really do. But after all this time of never being with anyone, I want to wait. "No. Not yet, Theon. Good night."

He sighs regretfully, but pulls back. "Good night, my queen." He then kisses the back of my hand like a perfect gentleman and walks to his room.

I turn and bolt into my own rooms before I can do something

stupid like change my mind and drag him in behind me.

Chapter 7

Theon stays at the castle with me, and we spend the time getting to know each other. Naturally, I end up having a conversation with Yemonja about my behavior with him at the ball, and the ramifications of agreeing to marry him so quickly. But I quickly remind her that it is my decision, and that I'll do what I like. I also tell her that we have no intentions of marrying immediately, and that I have time to get to know him before we make things official. No one knows yet anyway. No harm done if I decide not to go through with it. That seems to mollify her.

I instruct the staff to start working on preparations for the coronation and the wedding. I'm aware they can whip together an event quickly if need be, but I would rather them take their time, and be able to review and approve their plans. I need to be able to change things if something isn't to my satisfaction with ample time for execution.

The reality of the situation starts kicking in, and nerves and excitement flutter in my belly anytime I think of the fateful day approaching. The mere thought of ruling the kingdom with unmatched power, along with the idea of having Theon by my side as well as between my legs, causes my heart to flutter and my core to clench.

We spend as much time as we can with one another. I discover more about him and his race. Even though I grew up in this realm, demons aren't well educated, especially about the other species. I know the basics, but not much about their land or history. He's patient with me, teaching me everything I need to know, not only about his species, but about him as well.

I enjoy learning about him, and the more I absorb, the more fond I become. After that first evening, he maintains his distance, for the most part. A few weeks into our courtship, he attempts to get into my bed again, but I finally tell him that I'm a virgin, and that I would like to wait to be together until our wedding night. I don't know why it's important to me. It's not like I'm a prude; I know what sex entails. I grew up in a brothel, for Gods' sake. Perhaps that's the reason why. Because sex was always so commonplace and casual, I want the act to be something special, something I wouldn't give to just anyone.

He tells me he understands, although I can sense the disappointment in his demeanor. I almost ask if that's okay with him, but then remember myself. I am a godsdamn *queen*. What I say goes. Not the other way around. With that in mind, I tell him "Good" before giving him a quick peck on the lips and going about my business.

Weeks turn into months, and I feel myself becoming more and more refined with each passing day. I can also sense myself hardening and becoming colder. I haven't told anyone yet, but I've been dabbling in my demon powers. I've never used them much, only when I've needed to, but I justify the decision knowing I have to be as powerful as I can be. I will be the strongest leader this realm has ever seen. So, I begin small and subtle, gradually siphoning emotions and essence from various people bit by bit. I desire to make myself stronger and them weaker. After all, considering my background and deficiencies in the water, I need every advantage I can muster.

It doesn't take long to become addicted to the feeling of that small amount of power flowing through me, and I take more and more each time I feed. It's a constant struggle not to take more than I should. Take *everything.* I crave to have a might that no one else does. To be a force to be reckoned with. Not only that, but I relish leaving people in misery after and watching them suffer. I realize that sounds awful, but I was the one who was miserable for so long, that it feels empowering to be the one on top. There's also a cadence that purrs inside me when I feed off the darkness of others and witness their anguish.

I usually feed off the slaves, considering they are all replaceable. I don't want to feed off of people who I need. I'm careful not to feed off the emotions of those that I worry about damaging—Theon, Yemonja, and my council. I don't want to impair or alter their personalities. As loath as I am to admit it, I still need Yemonja.

As time goes on, I notice that every time I feed, my physical appearance heightens. I look healthier, more beautiful. My skin glows, my hair and horns shine, and blood floods my cheeks.

Theon and I fall more and more in love with each passing day. I find myself giddy with anticipation for the day that I'm not only crowned, but will have this man at my side permanently. We kiss every day, and I'm always tempted to take it further, but something stops me. I think it's the anticipation. Sex is never something I've desired until him. Now that I'm experiencing all these feelings, I want to bask in them and take it slowly. I'll never be able to have another chance at this, so I want to make it count.

One day, as we're simply relaxing and enjoying each other's company, he asks me something I haven't thought of before.

"How do you feel about the other demons? Would you ever bring any here? Are there any you were close to?"

I try to think of anyone from my past who I would want to see. I guess there are those who I would want to witness my success and power, and there are others who I didn't mind being around. But I had no one who I was close to. Although, it does make a certain sense to make my species appear more powerful. Their presence would elevate our race and perhaps others would think more highly of us. While I don't care about any demons I know personally, I do care about demons being viewed as powerful as a whole in our society.

I nod. "I think that's a good idea. I was never really close to anyone, but I wouldn't mind having other demons around."

A strange expression passes over his face, and I'm tempted to feed from his emotions to see what exactly he's feeling, but that would go against the rule I set for myself. It's gone in the next moment anyway, and I let it go.

The next day, I talk to Yemonja about bringing demons here, even appointing some as my personal servants. Even though I didn't originally think of this idea myself, I'm reluctantly excited to be around my own kind. I think their presence will bring comfort, and I look forward to showing them how far I've risen.

The demons start appearing throughout the castle within the next week, and something loosens in my chest as soon as I can sense them in my space. I don't quite understand *why* I'm reacting this way, but something in my blood calls out to them all the same. It's also refreshing that with my newfound status, and the fact that I'm elevating our species, they look at and treat me with near reverence. After all, none of our kind has *ever* been in a position of power before. I soak up their praise, getting drunk off of it.

I immediately assign two of the new arrivals as my lady's maids, wanting to be closer to them, even if I don't understand why. Their names are Elektra and Dalia. I'm grateful I don't know either of them. Having girls from the brothel here would be uncomfortable. As much as I would like them to see me as a ruler, I initially imagine it would be difficult not to fall into old roles and habits with them, letting them boss me around or demean me. The thought then makes me outwardly scoff. With my newfound position and power, I can't imagine letting myself be in that role ever again.

My lady's maids dote on me, and I can tell they're awed by the fact that a member of their species is now queen of the realm. I soak up their praise and excitement. As glad as I was to leave my old life behind, I have to admit that I missed embracing this demonic side of myself, and I'm glad to have her back. It's as if bringing them here has returned a slice of my soul to me.

After a few weeks of having Elektra and Dalia around, we become closer. It turns out they were raised in a similar situation to me, and were sent here before they had to actually serve in a sexual way. I open up to them about how my time here has been and what I've learned.

When we start forming an even closer bond, I share with them the fact that I've been feeding off those around me. Their brows rise in surprise, but they look delighted and intrigued.

"Is that something that you're comfortable with us doing?" Elektra asks.

"Absolutely. I want you both to be as strong as you can be. I need you to have my back in all things. But be discreet and keep it to yourselves. I don't need anyone else finding out and being upset that we're taking advantage of them. Also, don't feed off of other demons. I want us all to be seen as the strongest for once."

They nod enthusiastically.

Everyday Theon and I spend time together, either going on walks, reviewing plans for the wedding, or simply talking. I've thought about telling him about using my powers as well, but something always stops me. I don't think he would be pleased with the knowledge that I'm feeding off others, and things are going so well between us, I don't want to mess anything up.

"When are we going to announce the wedding, my little demon?" he asks one day.

The fateful day is now only two months away. Even though he's asking it as a question, I know he's really saying that we need to do it soon. He's right. The fae will need enough notice to make arrangements to come here, along with the rest of the realm. It's not mandatory for everyone to attend, but I imagine most will want to. It's an extremely significant event in our history. Not only is the last of Surseiha's line being crowned, but she is also marrying a member of a different race. The mermaids' reign is over. A demon and a fae will be on the throne now. That has never been the case.

"We'll announce it this week," I confirm.

He smiles, delighted. For a split second, I think I see a devious glint in his eyes but it's gone before I can confirm its existence. I shake off the unsettled feeling. This is Theon. *My* Theon.

With that decided, I speak to Yemonja about setting up the announcement. Her jaw clenches, but she nods. I can tell she's not pleased that I'm planning on getting married, especially the same night that I'm being crowned. She's of the mind that queens shouldn't marry. We can always conceive with someone when we're ready to further the royal line, but she hates that

I'm willing to share my power with another.

I don't blame her, but at the same time, there's a small part of me that feels relief at the fact that I don't have to handle everything myself. Making decisions for the realm won't rest solely on my shoulders, and that removes a bit of pressure. Maybe if I had been raised as she had I would feel differently, but I wasn't. Even with all the rigorous training I'm receiving, it's impossible for me to attain all of the knowledge that I would've acquired had I been born into the role.

We've had that conversation before, though, and she knows she won't change my mind, and bringing it up again will only anger me.

"I'll send out invitations to the realm for your coronation as well as your wedding. That's how we'll announce it."

I nod. "Within the week, Yemonja."

Her eyes smolder at the command, but her voice is pleasant when she speaks. "Of course, Your Majesty."

I'm aware that she hates when I give her orders. It only spurs the desire to do it more. It's never a bad thing to remind her of her place after all.

Nerves flutter in my belly when the invitations are sent out. It's official now. I don't plan to suddenly change my mind, but I never envisioned myself not only in this position, but married. In fact, my life is absolutely *nothing* like I could have ever imagined.

Weeks pass by quickly, and my excitement builds the closer we get to the day of the event. I can almost taste the power that's sure to follow, not to mention the pleasure. Heat flushes my skin and cheeks whenever I think about our wedding night. We still haven't done much, and I know Theon is frustrated about that, but he wisely abides by my requests. He understands that I want our first time to be something special.

The day my dress arrives, I squeal in excitement. And I am not a squealer. Ever. But it is the most exquisite piece of clothing I have ever seen in my life. For a full hour, Elektra, Dalia, and I all just stand and stare at the stunning creation. We debate on how to arrange my hair and makeup, and I find myself even more impatient for the day to arrive.

Chapter 8

It's coronation day. And my wedding day. The thoughts roll through my head on repeat as I prepare, my heart beating an excited pattern in my chest. With the amount of power I've been siphoning lately, my own emotions have been diminished. In fact I've felt a bit numb. Perhaps that should concern me, but I reassure myself that my dulled emotions are a small price to pay for the strength I'm gaining. Either way, waking up overwhelmed by my own emotions is, to say the least, quite overwhelming.

Dalia brings me my normal breakfast, but it's difficult for me to choke it down from the anxiety that's knotting my stomach. Elektra runs my bath, and the three of us spend the morning ensuring I'm as primped as possible. Every unwanted hair is removed from my body, and I'm scrubbed within an inch of my life. My hair is washed and brushed, a special tonic added to make it even more voluptuous and shiny than normal. My nails are clipped and painted, and the girls expertly cover the slight blackening that's begun at my fingertips. I think it's another symptom of my feeding, but I don't think about that now.

Dalia applies my makeup while Elektra arranges my hair. My face is shimmery and painted to perfection, and my hair is styled like a true queen, accentuating my horns. We want them to remember exactly what I am.

When Dalia and Elektra complete their tasks, it's finally time to don my dress. It's the most gorgeous piece of clothing I've ever seen, even more stunning than the dress that I wore for the last ball. The top is an all-boned corset encased in genuine gold. It has a V-neck and small tight-fitted sleeves with an almost nonexistent back that plunges to a deep V right above my backside. Once the garment reaches the hips, the fabric subtly flares out and flows loosely, barely kissing the floor. The gold pattern transitions a quarter of the way down my legs to white, the fabric bunched to look like flowers with a central golden pistil. I have a long train that trails behind me as I walk, and a slit up the front, allowing my matching gold shoes to peek out. Although the dress takes a ridiculous amount of time to put on, and the fabric in the torso restricts my movement greatly, the overall effect is stunning, making the effort worthwhile.

When I'm ready, I look in the mirror and I can't believe the woman staring back at me is the same one who grew up in a brothel. Although I am not that woman any longer, I realize, shaking my head slightly. She died the moment I walked into the waters of Mermacovia. I watch in morbid fascination as I harden even more. The last piece of my former self vanishes before my eyes. I should feel panic or sadness, but instead all I feel is power. And a thirst for more.

"You look beautiful, my queen," Elektra comments next to me.

Dalia nods next to her. She's less vocal in general, but is just as enthusiastic about my appearance. I smile at them, my excitement returning. I wonder how Theon will react to seeing me like this. I can't wait to see his face.

"Are you ready, Your Majesty?"

I take a deep breath and nod. Dalia picks up my train and we leave the room. I grip my bouquet tightly. It's arranged in typical mermaid fashion, containing shells, seaweed, underwater flowers that have been dried, and coral. I also had them add in some black lilies for a touch of me. I'm not primarily mermaid after all. My hands are sweating, and I feel like it's going to slip from my fingers at any second. My heart rate quickens as the nerves flutter in my stomach. I didn't anticipate getting nervous, but here we are.

The soft notes of my processional music start up outside the royal ballroom, and I inhale deeply before tilting my chin up and squaring my shoulders. The doors open, and I'm immediately overwhelmed by the number of people who are present. I've never seen this many people in my life. The crowd is spilling out into the foyer. *This is a good thing*, I remind myself. Let them see their new queen. Let them see the species they've neglected and essentially shunned rise up and become stronger and more powerful than them all. Anger tries to push through my elation, but I don't let it. I've already had too much taken from me. I won't allow this day to be tainted as well.

I block them out as I focus on my future husband standing at the end of the very long aisle. My stomach lurches again, but I push past the nausea. I want this. I stride forward, slightly faster than I should, but I don't care. Yemonja stands at the end of the aisle as well. She will be the one to marry us, and crown me as the queen. The irony isn't lost on me, and I come to the conclusion that she hates me in all likelihood, but once again, I don't give a shit. I hate her just as fiercely, I realize. She allowed our kind to be used as breeding animals.

Theon's eyes heat as he takes me in, and my core clenches in excitement for tonight. I'm ready. From the look in his gaze, he is too. Although, he's been ready since we met.

Yemonja starts speaking, but I'm too focused on my almost-husband to register anything she's saying. When it's time for our vows, Yemonja pours a liberal amount of red wine into a golden chalice in front of her before also picking up the dagger on the table.

"The time has come to cement your bond. Hold out your palms."

We do so, and I tense in anticipation. She cuts across my palm first and I hiss in a sharp breath. I hold my hand over the chalice, and watch in unnatural curiosity as the red liquid slowly drips into it. She cuts Theon next, and I sympathize when a wince crosses his face. His blood trickles into the glass next, and then Yemonja is handing it to me.

I look at Theon as I bring it to my lips. "I drink from us and welcome you into my body. I acknowledge that you will always be a part of me. From today until my last day, we will be joined in spirit." I drink deeply, the blood adding a slight tang to the wine. Surprisingly, it's not unpleasant. I expected to be more repulsed by drinking blood, but something inside me craves it.

I reluctantly hand the cup to Theon before I can drink the entire contents. He repeats the same vow, and finishes off the rest of the ceremonial drink.

Yemonja takes the chalice from him, setting it down before pronouncing us husband and wife. We kiss to seal our union, and the roar of applause is deafening.

Before we make our way back down the aisle, Yemonja has us kneel and face our guests.

"Do you both promise to hold the Kingdom of Queridian in the highest regard, only doing what is in the best interest of its citizens, swearing fealty to its residents and devoting yourselves to them until your heart stops beating?"

"I do," we both reply in unison.

She places my crown on my head first. It's as black as night, swallowing all light into its depths like a black hole. Its spires jut high, as if poised to pierce the sky above. The moment the diadem settles on my scalp, I can feel power rippling through me, causing a shiver to travel through my body in the most pleasant way. I nearly moan aloud.

Theon is next. His crown is similar to mine, but with more robust, masculine spires. A look of pure elation crosses his face, and I reach out to squeeze his hand. I know how he feels.

"Then rise. Queridian, welcome your new king and queen!"

We stand as the crowd erupts even louder than before, sinking to their knees in front of us. I soak in the praise. I've never felt this worshiped before. I could get used to this.

We return back up the aisle, and I drag Theon with me before anyone can approach us. I want a minute alone with him before we make our way to the reception. I pull him into the nearest room, slamming the door shut behind us and melding my mouth to his. He pulls me tight to him and I can feel his thickness pressing into my belly, and I moan against him. I'm suddenly *burning* for him.

I'm about to say fuck the reception and have him carry me straight to bed when there's a knock at the door. I groan in frustration against his lips.

"Your Majesties, the guests are waiting for you." It's Yemonja. Sometimes I really hate that bitch. I almost tell her that they can wait, but she chimes in again. "It would be incredibly improper and impolite to delay any longer."

I let out a low growl, but Theon chuckles. "It's okay, wife. We can have all the fun we want tonight."

"I'm going to hold you to that, husband."

"I look forward to it."

We step back and open the door to find Yemonja looking at us disapprovingly. We walk in front of her, not acknowledging her comment and attitude. I grasp my husband's hand and we stride into the reception hall.

Cheers erupt around us, and we wave and smile like we're expected to, even though the only place I want to be right now is in my bedroom with Theon. We sit at our head table overlooking the crowd. Champagne is located at every place setting, and someone in the crowd stands and shouts, "To the new queen and king!"

Everyone shouts the phrase and holds up their glasses. Theon and I clink ours together before taking a sip. The champagne is crisp and sweet on my tongue, and soothes some of the heat building inside of me. I do enjoy this. Ever since I've come here, I've discovered that I relish being the center of attention. I've never had the chance before, but now the worship feels comforting, soothing an ever-present ache I never realized existed.

The feast is promptly served, and it's the best thing that's ever touched my tongue. I'm glad the staff spared no effort for this. It makes the occasion even more special.

There are more toasts and shouts about how wonderful we are, and I soak it all in while at the same time keeping a mental note of who is vying for my good graces. I'll use them, but I won't trust them.

When the meal is finished, Theon and I stand and go to the dance floor. A slow, sultry song starts, and he pulls me into his arms. There's no one but us, and heat builds between my thighs with every sweep of our bodies against each other.

I'm so tempted to haul him from the room, but one look from Yemonja and I know that I can't quite get away with it yet. We take our seats, and people come up in droves to congratulate us. It's like the tide. A crowd of people sweep in, and just when I think it's dwindling, another group comes up. I sigh in frustration. I love the attention, but at the moment, I'm finished with it. I want only to get my husband alone.

When there's finally a break in people, I stand, taking Theon's hand. I'm done. Ready for bed. Among other things.

The group bows, although some are slower to do so. The drinks have been heavily indulged, and not everyone realizes what's happening.

My heart beats an excited, nervous pattern as we make our way to the bedroom. My palms start to sweat, but when he leans in to nip at my throat, wetness floods between my thighs.

As soon as we burst into my chambers—now *our* chambers, I suppose—the door slams shut and we're on each other. His mouth devours mine in a heated frenzy, making me feel like I'm on fire. My demon claws are out and he hisses when they shred through his clothing. I scent a touch of blood in the air, and I know I've scratched him. I can't find it in me to care. I feel like I've waited forever to have this moment with him, and nothing is stopping me now.

My dress is slightly more difficult to get off, and I would have him ruin it if it wasn't so beautiful and priceless. Some huffing and maneuvering later, I'm naked before him. That nervous flutter in my stomach is back, even as I watch his eyes heat as they take me in. My own gaze rakes his form.

My core pulses as I look at his hard length, but at the same time my stomach knots in anxiety. Will he fit inside me? I've heard about the male form, but I've never seen it in person. It's intimidating.

He holds a hand out to me, and I take it, allowing him to lead me to the bed. My heart beats faster as he sits me down and stands in front of me. My face is level with his groin, and I eye it with trepidation before looking up at his face.

"Open your mouth for me, my queen."

I do as he says, albeit hesitantly. I've heard about this before from the girls at the brothel, but it always sounded unpleasant to me. But I have made him wait to get me into bed, and it is our wedding night. I want to make it special for him.

His manhood brushes my lips, and he paints them with the wetness leaking from the tip. I dart my tongue out instinctively, and furrow my brows at the strange salty flavor.

"Wrap your lips around me, wife."

I do as he says, sheathing my teeth behind them before taking him into my mouth. He pushes forward slowly, although not as slowly as I wish he would. I'm surprised to find that with the exception of the liquid I tasted at the start, he doesn't have much of a flavor. It's basically just skin.

He groans above me even though I'm not doing much. I don't know *what* to do. Without warning, he grips my horns and his hips surge forward, making me gag as he hits the back of my throat. Tears spring to my eyes and I pull back, gasping for breath.

He looks down at me, frustration flaring in his eyes before they soften slightly. "I'm sorry. I'm just so excited to be with you. I wasn't thinking. Lie back."

I lean back, getting comfortable on the pillows and he crawls over me. I sigh in relief when he kisses me again. This I'm used to. This I can do. This I enjoy. And with our naked bodies pressed together and his weight covering me, it's much more pleasant.

After a minute or so, his mouth breaks from mine to trail down to my breasts. I gasp when he sucks my nipple between his lips. A slow and steady heat is building, and even though it's new, it's not unpleasant. His fingers explore my torso, and in the next moment they're trailing down my belly, heading south. I know where he's going, and I tense in anticipation.

When he grazes my bundle of nerves I almost shoot up off the bed. He chuckles against my skin as his fingers start stroking me before he moves them to my opening. I'm not sure if I want him to move on yet, but before I can say anything, he's pushing a digit into me. I cry out in surprise. I don't know what I was expecting, but it's different. He pumps into me a few times before he pulls it out completely.

"Are you ready for me, my little demon? I don't think I can wait any longer to have you."

I don't know if I'm ready or not yet, but I nod all the same. He's waited long enough. It's clear his patience is at its end.

He braces one arm next to my head as he reaches down with his other hand. I feel the head of his member brush against me and I tremble.

"Spread your legs wide."

I do. He holds himself steady and pushes into me slowly. I gasp at the fullness and the burn. Inch by inch he moves forward and I keep praying for him to be fully inside, but he still keeps coming. I close my eyes and he finally reaches resistance. He pushes forward a little more forcefully and breaks through my virginity. My breath hitches and I feel a tear roll down my temple and into my hairline.

Finally he's buried to the hilt. He groans in pleasure above me. I wish I could return the sentiment.

"Can I move? You feel so good." The pleasure in his voice

makes me relax a little, and the pain starts to ebb.

I nod. "Slowly."

He does as I ask and slowly pulls out of me and pushes back in just as languidly. Within a few strokes I begin to unclench a bit more, the pain almost gone now. I wrap my legs around his waist, feeling like participating instead of just lying here and taking it.

He growls approvingly and I bring his mouth back down to mine. I think that is still my favorite physical act. He obliges me as he increases his pace. I feel something starting to build in me. Nothing earth-shattering, but a slow heat creeping through my veins. I can feel my pelvis brush against his with every thrust and I wish he would just stay inside me and move his hips against that spot continuously.

The bed is banging against the wall now, and my breathing is coming faster. Theon is sweating and moaning above me, and I have a small moment where I'm repulsed. But in the next second it's passed, and I think I must've imagined it.

Before I can build anymore, Theon is stilling above me, burying his face in my neck as he empties himself inside me. I can feel him twitching in my body, making me notice the uncompleted feeling that's settled. He pulls out and I wince at the sensation. His seed spills out and onto the bedding, and I cringe at the wetness. No one mentioned this part to me. I can't say I'm a fan.

Theon collapses on the bed next to me, breaths heaving in and out. I get up and go into the bathroom, wanting to clean up. I use the toilet, spotting a bit of blood as I wipe, and wash up as best as I can before heading back into the bedroom. Theon is passed out when I return, looking thoroughly spent and satisfied. I can't help but feel envious. Not that I didn't like it. I did. It just wasn't as explosive as I was hoping it would be. I'm sure it'll just take time.

I lie down in bed next to my new husband. My breath whooshes out of me. I'm married. I'm a fucking *queen*. The reality is just now sinking in.

My thoughts continue whirling in a spiral with the events of the day and what my life is going to look like from here on out. Eventually my mind calms enough that I drift off to sleep.

Chapter 9

Something wakes me in the middle of the night. I don't know what it is, but a sense of unease is crawling over my skin. I have goosebumps and the hairs on the back of my neck are standing on end. It's like a cool breeze has swept in and chilled me to the bone.

I open my eyes to see Theon awake and hovering over me. I chalk up the feeling to just not being used to sleeping with anyone else. I smile up at him, but it turns into a pained gasp as I feel a sharp stab in my chest. I glance down to see a dagger protruding out of my torso. Is this a dream? A horrible nightmare? I look up at my husband again to see a cold, calculating look in his eyes and a sinister smile on his lips, and I know this isn't a dream.

"Why?" I bite out, barely capable of making any noise at all.

"So I can have the crown all to myself, of course. I'm sorry you were stuck in the middle, but this kingdom needs a real leader. Not some brainless, whorish servant."

Tears are pouring out of my eyes from both the pain and his words. I can feel darkness intruding on the edges of my vision, and I know I don't have long.

"I'll take good care of Queridian for you," he tells me as he twists the knife and shoves it deeper into my chest.

I take my last breath as I feel my heart give one final beat. Blackness descends.

Darkness. Everywhere. I float aimlessly, but I'm no longer numb. I can feel burning rage simmering through my veins, replacing the blood that had taken up residence there before. I can't place exactly why I feel this way. I don't remember why I'm here, or even where here is.

I wander. I need to find a way out of this godsforsaken place. I need to do something, but I can't put my finger on what. There's a driving need pushing me forward, and I know that if I could only remember and make sense of what it is then I'd be able to get out of here.

Minutes pass. Or maybe it's hours, days, weeks. I have no idea. I've lost all sense of time and self. The only thing I retain is my anger, and my sense of purpose. Frustration builds in me. Why can't I think? Why can't I remember?

I stop moving. It's the first time since I arrived here. I close my eyes, even though I'm not able to see anything in the dark to begin with, and take a deep, measured breath. I attempt to cool the fire in my blood. Maybe if I can settle down I can think properly.

I don't know how long I stay there, breathing and focusing, but eventually a memory surfaces. Theon's savage face above me, plunging his dagger into my chest. My eyes pop open on a gasp. He killed me. That motherfucker killed me. I can't believe it. So, I'm dead? Is that what this is?

Denial rises. No. I will not go out like this. With renewed anger and purpose, I push forward. I don't even know how to get back, but in that moment, I know that I will get there. Nothing will fucking stop me.

I tap into every ounce of power I stole and every bit of vigor pulsing through my veins. I run at full speed, pushing with all of my will and strength. Blackness shoves back at me, but I rage, batting it away with all of my might. Finally, finally, I see a light up ahead. I scream my defiance, surging into it with the last of my reserves.

My eyes pop open. I'm back.

I look down at myself. Blood covers the bed. More than any one person could survive. But the spot on my chest where there should be a gaping wound is *closed. I have elf powers*, I realize. It's the only possible explanation, and with it comes a certainty I can feel in my bones.

My eyes trace the room, intent on finding Theon and *ending* him, but he's nowhere to be found. My anger mounts again, higher and more fierce than I've ever felt. The mixture of fury and the lure of becoming more powerful than everyone who has oppressed me and my species for so long is overwhelming, and I can no longer deny or quell it. I dive headfirst into my demon powers, grasping at anyone and everyone I can feel nearby. I don't bother feeding off of only those that I don't care about. It's a weakness, I finally see, caring about others. With that thought, I feel the last of my dwindling compassion fly away like a leaf in the wind.

I feed off of *everyone*. Except my fellow demons. I want them to join me. I want them to bask in our power and never return to the humanity that plagues us now. I force my will onto them. Allure causes my skin to glow, and I can feel the influence in my veins. If I were in a different headspace, I might be shocked by the fact that I'm able to use another power, but I'm not. I bask in it. My mermaid powers are strong, even if I'm unsure how to use them. At the moment, my body seems to naturally know what to do.

Elektra and Dalia burst through the doors, eyes intently focused on me, ready to do my bidding. Within moments, my chamber is filled with every demon in the castle.

"Feed. Feed off of everyone and anyone. Join me in the darkness."

They close their eyes and moan in unison as they absorb the emotions of any and all within reach. Together, we plunge ourselves into the madness and numbness of our kind.

I test my reach, sending my influence out as far and wide as I can. I look for *any* with demon blood in our realm, pushing them to do the same. I'm amazed when I can feel them. I'm able to reach those in my territory. I can sense when their will joins mine. I have *all* the demons with me now. I have an army of soulless beings at my disposal.

I grin in malicious delight. I feed more and more until every trace of humanity and empathy is erased from my existence as if it was never there. I close my eyes and have a vision of the blackness on my fingertips creeping up my arms, and I know that one day it will engulf me. I welcome it. When I open my eyes and look down, it's already traveled past my wrists.

A ravenous emptiness builds in my stomach, and I groan in pain. I've never felt anything like it before. Almost thirst, almost hunger, but a burning in my throat. I feel a pressure in my jaw, and within moments I can feel fangs descend. *Vampire.* Blood. I almost lunge for the person closest to me, Elektra, but I stop myself at the last moment. I need to retain all of the demons I can and keep them with me. I *know* they will be my only allies. I can sense it. *Witch.* I have witch blood too.

I run into the hallway, naked as the day I was born, covered in blood, and not giving a single fuck. A slave squeaks in surprise as I rip the door open and grab her roughly, bringing her neck to my lips and biting down savagely. I moan as blood coats my mouth, and I swallow greedily, drinking and drinking. At the same time, I feed off her fear and panic. It's a heady combination, and I bask in it. I suck and suck, pulling her life force from her body and into mine. When the last drop of her blood hits my tongue, I release her, licking my lips in pleasure.

Fuck. There's no one more powerful than me, and no better feeling than what I'm experiencing right now. I walk back into my room, changing into a devastating black dress and putting my crown on my head. I want them all to see what I am now. I want Theon to see the beast he created.

"Meet me in the council room," I instruct my minions. I have a feeling I'll be able to teletravel now, too, since I'm clearly part vampire.

Before they can respond, I vanish, reappearing in the very place I told them to meet me. Just as I thought, Theon is here with the council, Yemonja included. Their eyes dart to me, shock and disbelief coloring them, and I smile, although there's nothing warm in it. It's full of malice and vengeance.

"Demonica." Yemonja is the first to speak. "What happened? How are you alive? Theon told us that he woke up to find you dead and covered in blood. We went to your room and saw it with our own eyes."

I turn my fiery gaze toward my husband. He looks nervous, but he has his mask back in place—the doting, loving spouse.

"My little demon, I thought I lost you," he says, standing and coming toward me, arms outstretched.

My rage intensifies, despite not realizing it was possible to feel even angrier at this point. A tide of violence washes through me. I'm overflowing, boiling over. I scream as I thrust my hands toward him. I stare down in shock as water bursts from them, encircling him. *Fuck me. I'm fae too.* That one doesn't please me as much, simply because of the creature in front of me, but I concentrate on the fact that it only makes me more powerful.

His eyes fly wide in surprise, but within a moment, he recovers, waving a hand and dispersing the water. Fuck. I forgot he had water magic too. I growl at him, shooting forward, claws extended, and slash at him. I'm like a wild cat backed into a corner. My nails rake down his face, drawing blood instantly, and the sight calms me just the barest amount. I wonder if with my elf power I can wound him in a way that's unhealable, even by another elf. I push my power into his face, digging my fingers into the cuts.

"Demonica! Calm down. You don't want to kill your husband!" Yemonja rushes me, pulling me off of him.

"Why wouldn't I when *he* killed *me*?"

Everyone looks stricken and doubtful between the two of us.

Theon's mask is firmly in place and I can tell he's going to lay the charm on thick even though he's crying out at the damage I've inflicted upon him. On the flip side, I'm sure I look insane. I'm covered in blood, my hands are black as night now, and I've fully embraced my demon side. I know they're not going to believe me. Even if I am their queen. Theon is their king now as well.

"Demonica, I didn't kill you," he shouts, sounding so convincing. There are tears running down his cheeks and emotion clogs his throat. "Someone snuck into our room while we were sleeping and killed you without me knowing. I woke covered in your blood. There are bloody tracks leading to the window. They clearly snuck in and murdered you."

If I were a weaker woman, I would believe him even though I know differently. I remember seeing his face above me as he shoved that blade into my chest. I look around and the council all look at me with concern and pity. They think I'm insane.

"How are you alive? When Theon came to get us, we went into your room to see everything. We were just about to come up to take care of your body."

"Not only am I Surseiha's descendant, but I also have witch, mermaid, fae, vampire, and elf blood. I healed myself."

Their eyes bug almost comically out of their heads.

"That cannot be," some old man I never bothered to learn the name of pipes up.

"You doubt me? When you see me alive and breathing right in front of you when you saw me dead not a half hour ago with your own eyes?"

He has nothing to say to that, and I release my allure, my skin glowing and shimmery. I flash him my fangs as I bring water forward again, swirling it around in my hand. They all look at me with stunned faces.

"So, what's it to be? I require this man's head at my feet. I am your queen."

Yemonja looks between the two of us. I know she hates me, but I also have Surseiha's blood in my veins. I don't know if that will matter to her now though. I see the way she eyes me more wearily than ever before. I can only imagine the picture I'm presenting to them.

"Technically, you died. Your heart stopped beating. You are

no longer the queen," she states firmly.

"Then it's to be war."

Before they can do anything, I feel myself shifting. Bones reform, and my size shrinks. I look down to see myself in a bird's body. I'm completely black with shiny soft feathers. I spread my wings and let out a loud croak. A raven then. I'm a mimic too. I have the blood of *all*.

If possible, they look even more shocked. I take off through the open window. I send out a persuasive signal to my fellow demons to leave the castle immediately. They meet me outside the walls.

"What are we doing, my queen?" Elektra asks, and I settle just the slightest at the title. At least some people still recognize I'm their queen.

"We're going to our territory and gathering reinforcements. They've dethroned me. I'm going to bring hell down on their heads."

Chapter 10

The journey takes nearly a week, but we finally arrive in our territory, *my territory.* I once again use my allure to summon every demon in the realm. I know it will take them days to reach me, but that's okay. For now, I step back into my old home at the brothel. Everyone I used to know is here, and instead of looking at me with disdain like they used to, adoration lines their features.

"My queen," they all say, bowing low. Word spread fast through Queridian when I was crowned, especially among the demons. It was unheard of for someone of our rank to suddenly be in such a position of power.

I smirk at them. I wish I could've experienced this when I lived here previously. "Prepare the nicest room for me. And get rid of all the patrons here. Your business is no longer open," I command the madam.

"Yes, my queen."

I could've gone somewhere else, but honestly, I wanted to make them grovel and wait on me hand and foot. What can I say? I'm a vindictive bitch. Even more so now.

Days pass, and I'm pampered as best I can be. Unfortunately, it's nowhere near what I became accustomed to with the mermaids, but Elektra and Dalia pick up as much slack as they can.

Eventually, every demon arrives. They wait outside the brothel that I've now set up as headquarters. I make them wait for me. I had to wait for them after all. When a sufficient amount of time has passed, I head outside to them.

I stand in front of the crowd, loving the look they all wear. They're eating out of the palm of my hand, and boy am I going to make them fucking scarf down everything.

"My citizens, there is false leadership now sitting on my throne. We march on Mermacovia to rectify the situation. I will not allow an imposter to steal my crown from me. It is unacceptable. Follow me into battle!"

That's all I need to say. The crowd erupts into shouts and war cries and then we're moving as a mass unit of hungry demons, their slighted queen in the lead. Power rushes through me. Honestly, it's *been* rushing through me since I brought myself back to life. I don't think the intensity of this high has diminished in the slightest. Perhaps if it had I would question how I instinctively understand how to use all my powers. Or I would struggle with how to wield them in some way, but I haven't faced any issues like that. Maybe I'm not using them in the "correct" way, but they clearly work, and that's all that matters to me at the moment. It could also be from the anger still coursing through my veins like fire.

It takes my army longer than I would like to reach Mermacovia and my castle. When we arrive, I'm unsurprised to see guards, more than usual, manning the entrance.

I turn to my group. "We're here to conquer. Feed, kill if need be. We *will* be victorious."

"Yes, my queen," they respond.

"Theon! Come and meet me in battle, you cowardly snake!" I shout, my voice echoing off the water.

The guards eye each other warily, and I flash them a demented smile. "You're willing to stand in front of him? You're willing to give your lives for a fae asshole that wormed his way into the castle?"

They give me dubious looks, as if they have doubts about their new king, but know there is nothing they can do about it.

"Join me," I tell them. I'll kill them when this war is over. Or feed on them. The only race I will have behind me after my victory is the demons, but they don't have to know that. Right now I need numbers.

They look at each other again, but there's a determination in their eyes that I know I won't be able to get around.

I'm about to attack them when Yemonja comes out. I scoff. Of course he doesn't come out to meet me. I knew he wouldn't, but I wanted everyone to see what a coward he is.

"Demonica, it doesn't have to be this way. Go back to your territory and let Theon rule. I know how hard it is to give up a throne. *Believe me.* But you're no longer fit to rule. And our laws don't allow you to anymore. Your reign died with you."

"And you don't care that your new king is the one who murdered me? That's fucking *treason!*"

"Demonica, we have no other choice right now. I cannot let you stay in power. Even though I am no longer the queen, I need to do what is best for Queridian. Look at yourself," she tries to reason with me. "You're clearly not stable. We can't have an unpredictable queen. And what have you done to yourself?" She gestures to my hands. "You've embraced your demon side and have been feeding? You know how dangerous that is." She finally looks at the others behind me and her eyes widen, taking in their blackening hands too. *"Gods. What have you done?"* There is genuine terror in her voice, and I feel it tainting the air.

I breathe in, sucking her fear and life force into me as I do.

"I did what should've been done long ago. I released my species from their cages, and allowed them to embrace their truest selves—the selves you've been making us repress! We were meant to rule. We are the most powerful, and that's why you've always put us down. That's why we've always been kept at the bottom. Because you *know* that we're dangerous. That we're the strongest force in this realm. No longer. *No longer will we cower underneath all of you!*" I shout, and my followers yell a war cry behind me.

We push forward and Yemonja pales, but she tries to stop me once more. This time, with her gift. *"Stop! Go no further!"* Her angelic voice rings out like a bell. Little does she know, my compulsion is stronger, and my demons are already under my thrall.

A cruel smirk twists my lips as nothing happens. Her eyes widen in shock and panic. I drink it all in as she turns and runs into the castle. More guards pour out of the building and block the way forward. I look behind me, making sure everyone is still with me. They are.

"Take care of them. Take out any you need to get into the castle."

"What will you do, my queen?" Elektra asks from my side.

"I'm going up to meet the council. And my husband." Without another word, I attempt to teletravel into the same room I did last time, but groan in frustration when I find my way blocked by a ward. As if they can keep me out with that. I roll my eyes at their pathetic attempts and shift into my raven form.

I release an almighty croak, letting my husband know that I'm coming for him and am out for his blood before taking off into the skies. I sweep into the same window I left out of the night

I awakened, but there's no one in here. Looks like I'll have to hunt for them. The thought is oddly thrilling, and I shift back, stalking forward, intent on finding my prey and ripping them to shreds.

I travel to my old rooms, finding everything cleared out and cleaned of all traces of my blood. Poor little Theon. He had too many horrible memories here. I shut the door with more force than necessary. If there were anything left in that room, I would destroy it.

I continue on my way before I can distract myself. I'm here for only one reason. Theon.

I check in the ballroom. No one. In fact, it's disturbing how empty the castle is. Even though I can *feel* others here with my magic, I just don't know where they are. I search room by room, and when I finally reach the throne room, I'm sure that's where everyone is. Theon will want to make a point of who's in charge now.

I burst through the doors with water magic, and they fly off their hinges and into the room. A scream erupts from inside and my blood heats, and except for my ever-present rage, the numbness that has settled over me is more apparent than ever. I have a realization that the rage will stay with me until I am no longer alive.

Theon sits on the throne just like I knew he would. He has a smug look on his handsome face, but I can see and feel the fear behind his facade.

"Aren't you happy to see me, husband?" I say loudly, walking in confidently.

"Of course, my little demon."

I sneer at the nickname. I used to see it as a term of endearment. It had warmed my heart, and my pussy for that matter.

Now, however, I see it only as a way to put me down. Make me seem less than him.

"Don't fucking call me that," I yell, my composure slipping.

He smirks. "Why not? I thought you liked it. Does it not make you wet anymore?" he taunts and I snarl at him, my fangs on full display. His eyes dart to them and I feel his trepidation. No one has ever encountered someone like me before.

"What's the matter, Theon? Are you scared of me?" I run my tongue over my new teeth.

He visibly swallows, but shakes his head. "Why would I be? There is only one of you."

I turn at his words, finding the council behind me. A small amount of fear creeps in on me. He's right. And with there being a member of every race on the council, I won't have the upper hand. All my powers can be counteracted. I shake it off. None of them have demon abilities. I open my senses to all of them and begin feeding. Even if it can't weaken them significantly, especially since I'm feeding from all of them simultaneously, it will still somewhat decrease their strength.

The main emotions I sense from them are anxiety, trepidation, and determination. I'm about to rush forward and attack—who first, I'm not sure—when I feel a blade piercing my back. I cry out in shock and pain before I hear Theon's voice in my ear.

"I killed you once. I can do it again."

He yanks the knife out and swiftly exits with the council, leaving me on my own.

Poor fools. They never learn. I heal the gash in my back. It's difficult because I don't know how to, but eventually I manage it. It takes me much longer than I was anticipating, and I'm sweating and breathing heavily by the time I've finished the repair, a good amount of my blood coating the floor. It also still feels tender and I realize I didn't accomplish it properly.

Dizziness overtakes me from the blood loss, but I push through it. I can find someone to sink my teeth into to take care of that problem.

I close my eyes and take a deep breath, trying to tap into my premonition to discover where they went. I don't know how to access my visions, but I focus on what I want to know and hope that's enough. It hits me a moment later. Underwater. They don't think I can follow them since I wasn't able to shift before. But I'm a mermaid now. I have to be able to breathe underwater...right?

Chapter 11

I run through the palace, although hobble is more like it. I push my senses outward, looking for any sign of life that's not underwater. I need to feed and replenish my blood before I can go after them. I sense a huge host of people outside defending the castle, and almost all of the mermaids are underwater, waiting for me to either die or join them. But I can feel a few people inside. Slaves. There would be no others who would be here when someone as demented as me was left to wander through these halls.

I head toward the kitchens. It makes the most sense to me. The closer I get, the stronger the pull, and my fangs tingle at the thought of being able to feed soon.

I burst through the doors and find three slaves cowering in the pantry. None of them are mermaids, which makes sense as to why they're up here.

"Stay completely still," I order them, allure coating my words, giving my speech a melody. For some reason, allure seems to come more naturally to me than my other gifts.

With them essentially incapacitated, I lunge. I want all of them. I don't *need* all of them, but that doesn't stop me. I sink my fangs into the first slave's throat, delighting in the combination of her blood and emotions. I gorge myself, draining her completely before finishing off the other two. Power floods my system, and I bask in it, my skin glowing like a star while I recharge and heal myself as much as I can.

Feeding like this is interesting, and not something I've ever experienced, with the exception of right after I was awakened, and I was too consumed by bloodlust to really appreciate it.

Being so immersed in your victim's despair, as well as being in physical contact with them and draining their life force on multiple levels, the feeding is extremely more intimate. I can see their life flashing before my eyes, and I revel in every memory and emotion I unearth, each as delicious as the last.

When I've finished my meal, and I have three dead bodies lying at my feet with horror etched on their pretty faces, I head to the section of the castle that I never travel to.

I strip out of my clothes, with the exception of my crown, and dive into the water. Runes start to glow on my skin, and almost immediately I feel a pull deep in my gut. I follow it, knowing that my mermaid will be on the other end. I can feel her calling to me like a siren.

When I reach her, I watch in fascination as my body transforms. It feels different than my raven. I can't explain it. My bird is more *animalistic* for lack of a better term, but my mermaid is *primal.*

My tentacles—*tentacles*—are red and black and slender. I have matching black-and-red-tipped scales on my forearm, sharp enough to cut, and when I feel my teeth with my tongue, I taste blood from the severeness of my canines slicing it open.

I grin in wicked delight as I shoot forward with unnatural speed. I'm on the hunt now, and I'm thirsty for blood. A small part of me wants to finally explore this part of the castle, but I don't have time for that now. When I reclaim my throne I'll have all the time in the world to do whatever the hell I'd like.

I swim fast, but try to stay out of sight and stick to the shadows. I don't want them to know that I'm able to swim and breathe underwater. I discover the council's location ten minutes later. This section of the castle is actually bigger than the land portion, which makes sense since we're in Mermacovia after all.

They've strategically barricaded themselves in a grand room, likely thinking they'll have more space to fight me if I did somehow manage to come down here. *Cowards*, I inwardly hiss. I did indeed find a way here, and they're going to regret it, I think as I take in my new impressive form.

Theon is being fed air by Yemonja, and a small spark of jealousy rips through me to see her mouth on his. Without thinking, I screech, powering forward and making myself known. I grip her by her hair and yank her off of my husband. My teeth are descending on her throat before I even realize what I'm doing. Before they make contact, however, I'm hauled backward, claws digging into my skin. I snarl and snap, throwing both mermaids off me with feral force. They crash into the walls and I surge forward again. Yemonja is ready for me this time, however.

She meets me in a heated battle in the middle of the room. Our claws slash, teeth gnash, and tails and tentacles whip as blood coats the water around us. My heart beats faster and my lungs work harder the longer we battle, and I'm surprised to find that we're fairly evenly matched. I also vaguely realize that someone has taken over giving breath to Theon.

Unfortunately, Yemonja has had much more practice than I have, not only in her mermaid form, but also in the water. Fortunately, I have my newly acquired powers to counteract that. I'm able to manipulate the water when I need to either push her away or pull her to me. I also have my witch senses to alert me when she's about to deal a fatal blow. I'm unaware of exactly how long we battle. It could be minutes or hours, but we're both waning, clearly spent and exhausted.

I'm growing impatient, and when I go to rush her, intending to cut to the chase and rip her fucking heart out, she whips her tail out, knocking me off my path, and the blow makes my brain fuzzy. Before I can recover, she's on me, pinning me to the floor, her teeth on my neck. Just as I feel her start to bite down, a mermaid comes rushing into the space, mentally shouting to stop.

Three more mermaids come forward and pin me down. They had stayed back and let us duel without interfering, but now there's clearly something else going on. Yemonja looks at them expectantly and with no patience for interrupting her kill shot.

The demons are overtaking the castle. They've killed all our guards and are starting to sweep through the city.

Yemonja looks down at me, a sneer painting her beautiful lips. I tilt mine up in response. My minions will kill and feed off the whole fucking city and she knows it.

She looks to Theon. He points at me and then points toward the upper section of the castle. She nods, and they roughly escort me up. We reach the stairs and instead of letting me walk, they drag me. I shift back, trying to get my legs under me, but they're moving too quickly.

When Theon is above water, he takes a deep breath and I can tell he's relieved to be able to breathe without assistance. Yemonja quickly fills him in on the conversation he wasn't able to hear while we were underwater.

I'm delighted to see that there are slash marks scored across his face. They're healed, but it looks like I was able to at least prevent them from healing the scar tissue. I give him a demented smile.

"What do you want, Demonica?" he cuts to the chase.

"Your head at my fucking feet," I spit back at him.

"Be reasonable, Demonica. What will it take for you to leave and take your demons with you?"

"There's nothing you can fucking give me. Unless it's my crown back and you six feet under."

"What if I could give you a different kingdom?"

Everyone's heads snap to him.

"What the hell are you talking about?"

"There's another realm."

Gasps erupt around the room. I narrow my eyes at him. I've never heard of such a thing.

"It's true. Yemonja discovered it years ago and told me about it before you arrived with your demonic army. It's desolate, but you could take your demons there and leave us in peace. We never have to see each other again."

"What makes you think I would want some shit-hole realm?"

"Because you and your demons would get to leave here alive, and you'd be able to still rule."

"But my demons are winning. Why would I give up the fight now?"

"Because *you* are not winning. If you don't take this deal, we will simply kill you and hope that is enough to end this."

Fuck. *Fuck.* He's right. Yemonja was about to rip my throat out and I'm spent. There's no way I could win against them all now, and I can't be sure of awakening from the dead for a second time.

"How do I know you'll hold up your end of this once I call my army off?"

Theon's lips thin in frustration. *Fucker was planning on killing me anyway.*

"We will make a magical pact. If you swear that you and your demons will go to this other realm, I promise that we will not kill any of you if you swear to do the same." He holds his hand out and I eye it warily. I don't trust him for a single second, but what other choice do I have?

"I want the slaves."

His eyebrows rise. "The slaves? Which ones?"

"All of them. We need people to feed off of now and I won't be stranded without a food source." *Technically, we won't die without being able to feed on others, but it will be difficult to stop now that we've started. Not to mention it will allow us to live longer.*

A growl builds in his throat. "Only if you allow us to put up a ward around Queridian. I will need a full demon to take blood from to perform the spell. You or anyone with demon blood will not be able to return here."

"Will it prevent others from coming into *my* realm?"

He shakes his head. "No. Just demons from entering Queridian."

I shake my head vehemently. "I don't like that. As soon as you want, you can bring a group together and come to me and take my kingdom from me. *Again.*"

He scoffs. "We won't be doing that."

I think for a moment. "How about this? I will allow you to build a ward. But only one that's dependent on the species staying separated."

His brow furrows. "What does that have to do with anything?"

Besides the fact that I want everyone here to be as miserable as possible, I'm also hoping that they will slip up and I'll be able to sneak back in to take my revenge. I can't tell him that though. So I devise another reason that holds some legitimacy—an inclination vaguely hinted at by my premonition senses. "I don't want to be defeated again. I *will* not be defeated again. I know that all the species allied together could best me, but especially if there were to be another like me. I won't allow it."

"That's impossible. There can be no others like you because you are taking all with demon blood with you. We will no longer have conduits," Yemonja pipes in finally.

"For now. As we've discovered, there are other realms. Who's to say that another race won't show up at some point and fill that void?"

Her mouth snaps shut.

"Those are my conditions. Give me the slaves and segregate. If you do that, we will leave, and you'll never have to deal with us again."

Theon looks at his council warily. A few shake their heads, but don't say anything. Yemonja, however, hardens her features, glaring at me. It's strange how much our relationship has changed. Even though I've always known she doesn't like me, she's always been respectful. She's always *had* to be respectful. That's no longer the case. Her distaste for me is even more obvious now.

"Get rid of her, Your Majesty," she spits, addressing Theon while never taking her eyes off me. "The demons have been a plague in our realm for too long. This is your chance to be done with them once and for all."

Wow. If Theon hadn't killed me and tricked his way into taking my crown, Yemonja would be putting up a good fight for my least favorite person ever.

I look at my husband. Determination lines his features as he nods. I vaguely wonder what their relationship will look like once I'm gone. Maybe they'll turn on each other and do my job for me by killing one another. That would make me deliriously happy. Well, as dementedly happy as I can be in this state I suppose.

"Deal." He reaches his hand out and I clasp it. Yemonja states the terms of the bargain we're striking first before hovering her hand over ours and murmuring quietly, and I feel magic bind between us. *Again.* I hate being bound to this man in any way, but it's unfortunately necessary. If I'm lucky, they'll mess up and I'll be able to take advantage of it.

As soon as the spell is finished, he speaks up again. "Now, call off your army."

I huff, but do as he says, closing my eyes and reaching out to all of them. *Stand down.* At once, the clamor outside dies. I didn't even notice the background demonic cacophony and screams of their victims until it suddenly went silent.

"Call one of your full-blooded demons here so we can perform the spell," Yemonja instructs.

I growl at her low in my throat. I've always hated following her orders, but now more than ever I want to rip her fucking head off.

"Do it," Theon snaps.

I snarl at him too, but obey. The sooner this is over, the sooner I can be out of his presence and in my own realm.

Dalia arrives moments later. She bows to me, and her eyes never leave mine. I know she'll do whatever I instruct. "Hold out your arm to them, Dalia."

She does so immediately, and I eye Yemonja warily as she grabs a knife.

"Only take what you need. You will *not* kill her or take more than you have to for the spell. Do you understand me?"

"Why of course, *Your Majesty*," she sneers disdainfully. Before I can do anything for her insolence, she slashes the blade across Dalia's arm, making her hiss through her teeth. Blood drips from her wound and into a bowl.

As soon as she releases Dalia, I snatch her and heal her arm. I then grab Yemonja by her arm, digging my blackened claws into her arm, drawing blood myself. Blood for blood and all that.

She sucks in a sharp breath, but doesn't react beyond that. "If you ever harm one of my kind again, the deal is off, and I will fucking *end you.*"

A spark of pleasure lights in my chest when I feel her fear and can see it so plainly in her eyes, even though she's trying to disguise it. It's no use against me. I close my eyes and breathe in the emotions I awaken in her.

"I can taste your panic. It's so delicious," I whisper in her ear, moaning as power runs through me. She shivers in response and I lick a line up her neck.

Before I can bite down and taste her blood, Theon slams a hand on my shoulder.

"There will be none of that. We struck the deal. It's time for you to gather your people and leave."

"I will first be collecting my things."

He narrows his eyes at me in suspicion. But at this point, we will literally have nothing in this other realm. He seems to realize that at the same time I do. The thought would scare me if I could feel anything besides my rage and bloodlust.

"Fine." He calls two guards forward along with one of my previous mermaid servants. "They will escort you to where your things are being held, and Crissa will help you pack everything to hasten your departure. It can't happen soon enough," he scoffs.

I smile cruelly at him, stroking a sharp claw down his cheek. "You want to be rid of me so soon, husband?"

He shivers in what I can feel is reluctant lust and anxiety. "Yes."

"Are you sure you don't want to plunge into my body once more? You enjoyed it so much last time. You spilled your seed into me before I could even climax. I have to assume that means you liked it?"

He visibly swallows and tries to shake off the attraction he still feels for me. Anger burns in his eyes, too, at the insult to his manhood.

"I think it would only be fair for you to give me an orgasm of my own this time, don't you agree?"

I let out a sliver of my allure and his eyes flare as he rakes his gaze over me. I trail my finger down his chest, pressing just enough for him to feel a bite of pain, but not enough to break the skin. He inhales sharply.

"I think that sounds fair."

"Is that something you want? To feel your wife's body once more before you banish her to a desolate land?"

"Yes." His voice is husky and filled with want.

I bring my lips just a breath from his. "Well, this"—I pause, as close as I can be without actually touching him—"you can't have. Know that from now on, I will be getting my pleasure from anyone and everyone I want. My followers will gladly serve me and give me everything I could ever dream of. Meanwhile, you will never be satisfied like you were inside of me. You will not find the pleasure your body craves so badly, and every person you let into your bed will be as unsatisfying as you were for me."

With that, I pull away from him and he groans helplessly as I turn my back on him. I smirk deviously. I don't know if I have the power to bestow a curse on someone or not, but that felt a whole lot like I did. And now, even if I wasn't actually able to, he will be thinking of that moment whenever he takes a new partner into his bed. Sometimes mind games are better than any curse.

Chapter 12

Two guards escort me to where my belongings are being kept. Dalia and Crissa follow behind me. We enter the storage room, and my things are piled in the corner haphazardly, as if they belonged to a peasant instead of a queen. I scoff but make my way forward, the two ladies on my heels.

"We'll be right outside. Don't try anything funny," one guard says to me with false bravado.

They close the door and the three of us start packing. We work in silence for the first few minutes, but eventually Crissa looks at me and beckons me to her.

My brows knit in curiosity and confusion, but I oblige. She has me intrigued.

"Your Majesty." I suck in a harsh breath at her whisper. I didn't know anyone still saw me in that light. "I hate to see you go. You are the rightful heir, and I've thought so since it was announced. I'm horrified he stole your crown from you, and I'm not the only one. I will help the true queen in any way I can. I don't know what, if anything, I *can* do, but I am your willing servant."

"Thank you, Crissa. For now, gather what followers you can. I have every confidence the bastards won't be able to abide by the stipulations I set, allowing me to return quickly. I will need all the support I can get."

"Of course, Your Majesty."

After that, we resume packing in silence, not wanting to be overheard. After all, Crissa will be of no help to me if she's dead.

When my belongings are securely packed and gathered, I'm escorted from the palace. *My palace.* Yemonja comes with us because she is the only one who knows of the portal's location. It's astonishing how many people are following behind us. Not only do we have all of my demon subjects in our entourage, but every slave in the local area has been summoned and collected to depart to our new home. A good portion of them carry all the belongings we're able to bring with us. The remaining slaves of the realm will need to be gathered and transported. I would worry about Theon and Yemonja holding up their end of the bargain, but for the magical pact that will force their hand.

I think of something then. A loophole I could exploit. "Yemonja. I just realized something."

She reluctantly looks at me. "What?"

"You won't be able to have slaves anymore."

"Well, not the ones you're taking, obviously, but we will be able to obtain more."

I smile vindictively at her. "No. According to the deal we made, any slaves belong to me. So, if you were to get more slaves, you would be bound to bring them to me."

Her face pales.

"Make sure to tell my darling husband that when you return, will you? I want to make sure I'm given what I'm owed."

She huffs and storms off ahead of me. I love her unchecked reactions. It's so delightful knowing how much I'm getting under her skin.

We continue traveling on foot across the island until we reach a cluster of boats on the far side. The mermaids hardly ever use the boats, but because they're on an island, other species need to be able to reach them as well. We occupy every single boat here, and I know she will have to make multiple trips back and forth in order to transport everyone.

We set sail, but it's not a far ride. Yemonja signals us all to stop before stripping off her clothes and diving into the ocean.

She pops her head up when none of us follow her. "Well, come on!"

"You're forgetting that they can't breathe underwater."

She rolls her eyes at me. Very queenly, I think. "It's not far to swim. They won't need to breathe."

I don't trust her, but I also don't have much of a choice. I strip out of my own clothes and jump into the water. My other demons will carry my belongings for me. I shift and delight in the feeling of my tentacles stretching.

"Show me first. I don't trust you."

She huffs, but dives beneath the surface and I follow her. Sea life surrounds us, but it thins out the closer we get to our destination. I can see where we're headed, and she's right. It's not far under, and I know the others will be able to reach it in one breath. Underwater caves.

Trust me now? Yemonja asks in mind speak.

Trust? No, but I do see that they'll be able to make it.

We turn back and I instruct everyone to hook up all the chests to some rope so they're able to easily transport them through the water.

When they get it set up, we head back toward the caves.

Once we enter, I'm astonished at the open air space above us. I wonder if it has something to do with the tide. I climb out of the water and onto the cave ground. Nausea hits me strongly, and I sway. I can already tell this isn't going to be pleasant.

Yemonja stands in the center of the space and holds her arms out wide. She speaks words I don't understand, and before I know what's happening, stones appear out of nowhere, shimmering into existence onto the cave floor. They fill the space and begin glowing. There are symbols carved into their surfaces that I don't recognize, and suddenly the cavern hums with more power than before.

"What did you do?" I ask her.

"The stones need to be present for you to travel to the other realm. When one person travels through a portal you need a stone to channel the energy with runes for the magic to recognize. Usually you just need to hold the stone to travel through, but with so many of you, this will be much easier. Since the space is filled with them, it overpowers the portal, making it possible for a group of people to travel through."

Interesting. She faces where the portal is now shimmering to existence in front of us. "Typically you can't see the portal, but with so many stones present, the magic is brought to the forefront."

While her back is turned, I grab the smallest stone I can find. It's still larger than I would expect, but I'm able to shove it into my pocket without her realizing. Sounds like I'll need one to get back. And believe me, I *will* come back.

"What's the name of this other realm?" I ask.

"It doesn't have one."

"Well, I should name my new kingdom then, shouldn't I?"

She gives me a bland look.

"I'll call it Domonia. If you want to call it the Domain of the Dead, that's fine too. None of us have souls anymore." I flash her a wicked grin and she pales at the declaration, but recovers quickly.

"After you, *Your Majesty*," she says my title in that condescending tone again, covering her uneasiness with bravado.

Before she can react, I shoot my hand out and snatch her eye right from her socket. Blood and gore coat my fingers and she screeches in pain and outrage. I bring my other hand to the same socket and pour that *un*healing magic into her. She shrieks again and tries to pry my hand away with both of hers, clawing at my arm, but I hold steady. If I'm lucky, the elves won't be able to heal this at all and she'll have to wait for it to heal on its own.

"You *bitch*," she yells at me, but I ignore her and stride forward, my head held high with my prize from her gorgeous face still clutched in my palm. I will walk into my new kingdom no other way.

As soon as my body makes contact with the magic, I'm pitched forward. My body twists, and for a second it feels like the world is upside down. My stomach lurches, but all at once it stops. I'm on the other side.

Domonia, my new kingdom, awaits. And it's just as black and ugly as my heart.

Chapter 13

I survey the desolate land around me. It's bleak and gray, a sharp contrast to what I just left behind. There are some plants, but they're ominous looking, as if survival is a struggle in this climate.

There is a sun overhead, but it's much smaller and farther away than on Queridian. As such, the climate is cooler. The sky is swallowed up by dark clouds that blot out what little sun there is. Domain of the Dead indeed.

My followers begin to arrive behind me, and I move forward to make room for them. Without waiting, I start walking. I need to find a good place for us to start settling down. I'm glad that I have enough people who can start working immediately. I wonder briefly how upset my people would be with me if I hadn't warped their minds. Would they be vengeful? Vindictive? Would they resent me for having them banished? No doubt, but I have no feelings left to care.

I will command my subjects to craft a temporary shelter to house us quickly. Eventually, I'll need a castle. I am the queen after all. Or maybe I should start calling myself an empress? Or maybe even a deity. With the power I contain, I'm basically a goddess now after all. I make all of the rules now; I *command* here. My power is unmatched by any other being in this realm.

No one will take my crown from me again.

I debate testing out some of my powers now that we're safe. I'll need to practice since I won't have proper tutelage. For now, I concentrate on shifting into my raven form. It takes me a few minutes, but I'm eventually able to manage it. I spread my wings, let out a croak, and take off.

After some exploring, I find the perfect spot for us to settle down. It's not *pretty* exactly, but it is beautiful in a dark, depressing sort of way. There's a large cliff that overlooks the dead trees and forest below. A twisting black river runs through the trees, and a bird caws ominously in the distance. I also hear ferocious-sounding animals in the distance. I can't tell what they are, but growls and howls pierce the rapidly impending night air.

I smile. It's a realm full of predators, but I'm the most dangerous one here. This might not be so bad after all.

"Start building," I order. Luckily, we were able to take some essential tools with us. Not as many as I would have liked, but enough to be able to make it work. We can craft more of what we need as well.

I watch as groups of demons rush off to do my bidding. I appoint a dominant-looking demon to manage and direct the first group of slaves. While they are primarily here for feeding, there is no reason not to use them for labor, as long as they aren't overworked. We don't want them dying after all. Additionally, the manual labor will increase their desolation, and will make the feeding even more delicious and potent.

One group chops down trees and gathers wood, another rounds up any food or water they can find. Of course we don't know what will be safe to ingest yet, but that's what testers are for. Who they are, I don't care. I'm bound to lose both demon subjects and slaves from these tests, and I'm not shocked to realize that it doesn't bother me in the slightest.

In the meantime, I command another group to create a comfortable spot where I can relax while my kingdom begins to take shape.

Months pass. My castle is progressing from the plans we created, implementing local materials as best as we could for ease of construction. We've had to improvise and make do with what is available to us in this new realm, which has also prompted new discoveries and inventions with interesting results. The demon community has begun to thrive now that they are released from the yoke of Queridian, to my surprise and satisfaction. Don't get me wrong, it's been an adjustment, but we're settling in, and something about this realm suits us.

Every day I attempt to travel back through the ward leading to Queridian, and every day I fail. I sigh. They've already lasted longer than I anticipated. I didn't think the segregation would stick—I thought they would last only a few weeks. Fuckers are more persistent than I gave them credit for. Slaves are still trickling through, but are much less frequent now.

I've had to put a restriction on feeding. We found out very early that feeding on someone too much and too often causes them to die too quickly, and we can't afford to be killing off our food source. We need to make sure these people live as long as possible. That is how we plan to live forever after all. Especially me.

Months turn into years. Years turn into decades. Decades turn into centuries. My theory has been proven correct about us being able to live and stay young as long as we're able to feed off others' life forces, but to my disappointment, I'm still unable to get through the wards. I used to try every single day, but over the years, my attempts have become less and less frequent. I still possess the stone that I stole from Yemonja, and I take careful pains to ensure that nobody knows of its existence. If something were to happen to it, I would really never be able to return. My need for vengeance still burns hot, even after all of these years. It feeds and sustains me throughout our colorless existence in this realm.

Then one day, I start to feel the winds shift—the wards are changing. Somewhere, the races are coming together. I can sense that it's not a large group, and not enough to break the magical covenant and allow me through, but it's something. I resume my frequent attempts to get through the barrier. Every time I push it's slightly more degraded. I push with all my might, but the wards still hold.

Months slip by again. Then years. Still only minute incremental declines. Although the wards do continue to gradually weaken, I've observed it's occurring only in one spot— essentially in the middle of Domonia. I don't understand the significance. Is this near the area races are mingling or is the weakening caused by something else entirely?

Whenever I try to concentrate on what could be happening, the cause slips further from me until suddenly, during one such attempt, a vision slams into me. There's a group living in a set of caves that are comingling with each other, living peacefully and away from the eyes of others. The caves must have somehow been shielding their presence from my vision. I wouldn't be surprised if they were rebelling against the royals and laws.

Until one day, I feel the wards weaken so significantly that they're hanging on by the smallest thread. I push and push toward the bounds of the magic, hoping to break through, but nothing happens. Fuck. I'm so close. Maybe it just needs one more day to degrade further. Maybe I'll be able to break through tomorrow.

The following day I come back to the depleted area, stone in hand. I walk up to the portal that I know exists here. Except the wards aren't weak anymore. They're as strong as the day I arrived. The knowledge hits me—the group disbanded. They segregated once more. My chance is fucking *gone.* Centuries of checking, pushing, probing for *nothing.*

I roar my rage to the sky. My power explodes out of me in every direction, water shooting from my palms, skin shining and flaring like a star in the sky, before I shift into my raven. I cry out into the night, flying far and wide, circling back to my palace. There's nothing left for me to wait out here for anymore. My chance is gone.

Chapter 14

Crissa

I watch my queen and her demons leave with a heavy heart and anger burning inside me. She is Surseiha's heir. It doesn't matter that she died. She came back. She brought herself back to life. And now, not only is she gone, but Yemonja isn't even ruling either. We're stuck with the filthy fae man who none of us can stand. Well, at least I can't.

In the months following her departure, I bide my time. I have to make sure not to draw any unnecessary attention to myself. The powers that be need to believe that everyone is happy my queen is gone. Once they relax and think they are safe, I start gathering support for the true queen. At first I broach the subject with only those I'm close with. I'm surprised when there are more people who were upset to see her banished than I thought there would be. In fact, our beliefs seem to be the majority opinion, but everyone has been so afraid to speak up after what happened. We keep it close and quiet, subtly probing others and forming a tight-knit unit.

Right now we don't have any sort of plan, but I know the more of us there are, the better chance she'll have when she returns. I don't even know what we can do to help her come back, but I'm doing what she asked of me.

I keep a close eye on the king. Of course as soon as Demonica is gone, he takes lover after lover to his bed. I'm pleased to see, though, that he never looks satisfied. He has bags under his eyes, and despite the fact that he's now the sole ruler, he seems more stressed and tense than ever before. Serves the asshole right for killing my queen. I know the story he's told everyone, that someone snuck into their room on their wedding night and killed her. I don't believe one word of it.

On the opposite side, Yemonja has turned into a pariah. The mermaids have shunned her. She remains at Theon's side, offering him advice and worming her way into any decision and meeting she can, attempting to make herself important once again. But the fact is, we've seen what she's done. She betrayed our queen. Surseiha's rightful heir. She had her eye ripped from her face as a reminder of her treachery and now everyone can see the shame that stains her. If there's one thing mermaids covet more than power, it's beauty, and she is now hideous. The damage from her eye continued down into the side of her face, tainting and sagging her appearance with her betrayal. The unhealing magic my queen poured into her festered, turning the skin into a sickly gray color. Although the gruesome wound should be healed by now, I can see how unsuccessful her attempts have been to repair it. I smile in savage satisfaction every time I see her struggle to cover the disfiguration.

As the months pass, there's more upset in the realm, especially in Mermacovia. We don't like the changes that are being made to our beloved Queridian, and we all know the reason behind the turmoil is the bastard on the throne. Those who had slaves are also furious that they were forced to give them up without an alternative. No one in Queridian is able to have slaves anymore because they are magically bound to immediately give them over to the demons. The unrest is obvious, and it's clear that those in charge are growing anxious. They give more speeches about how they saved us from a demented ruler, and how they flushed out the scum of our realm.

When the king decides he no longer wants to live in Mermacovia anymore, I rejoice. I can stay here and avoid his influence and presence completely. The realization then dawns on me—I told myself I would keep an eye on him for my queen. Damn it. Not to mention that he's exiling everyone from the palace. He has started construction on a new one in his own territory. He thinks it's only fitting since the fae are the rulers now. Why should he have to stay here among the mermaids?

I sneer in disgust. The fae have always been pretentious assholes, and now they have the title and position to back it up. It's only going to get worse. We move out of the castle, and my heart sinks when I see it emptied.

He has the upper portion burned. I comfort myself with the knowledge that we will still have the underwater section. For some reason he doesn't care about that area as much, and I have a feeling it's because my queen wasn't able to inhabit that portion when she lived in it.

Even though the underwater portion still exists, entry is forbidden. It's not being closely monitored, but everyone has been too terrified to go near it.

When the day arrives for a mandatory announcement, my stomach sinks with dread. I don't know what they're planning on telling us, but I know it's going to be something horrid. I can feel it.

I make a split second decision as everyone heads to the main square for the announcement, and go in the opposite direction, heading instead to the sea. I hide from everyone, not wanting to be seen. I know I'm probably going to get in trouble for missing this, but maybe if no one sees me then I'll be able to avoid punishment.

I swim faster than I ever have before, heading for a group of caves that are fairly unknown. I hide there for hours. I have no idea how long the announcement will take, but I figure it's better to be safe than sorry.

When I feel like an ungodly amount of time has passed, I sneak out. Mermaids are back in the water and going about their daily lives. I sigh in relief and head back to my own.

Days pass. Things are strange. I've met with a few people in my group who are loyal to our queen, but whenever I try to talk to them about any of it, they seem confused. When I specifically mention our queen by name, they have no idea who I'm talking about. My anxiety grows with every individual I talk to. Something is very wrong. They don't even know what or who demons are. How do none of them remember an entire *species* even existed here?

It dawns on me eventually. The announcement wasn't an announcement at all. They erased everyone's memories. I know it. That means they're going to find out sooner or later that I still remember. I have to document all of this. I don't know if anyone will ever come across the information that I leave, but I have to try.

I write down everything and anything related to the demons, Demonica, and what happened between her and Theon. I leave nothing out. I waterproof the book with a spell every mermaid knows. Then, in the middle of the night, when I'm sure there will be no one around, I take my journal to the old underwater palace. I can think of nowhere else to hide it. I don't want it found by the wrong people after all.

The library is still virtually untouched. All the books have a water resistant spell on them so they will remain undamaged. There's an abundance of knowledge and information here that will stay here. The thought is depressing. I sneak the book into a free space in the stacks. I have to believe that somebody is going to find this one day. I realize that now, this is the only thing I can do to serve my queen.

In the morning, I'm approached by a guard. My heart sinks. They know I know and they're coming for me. I reluctantly follow them, having no choice now.

"Why did you not come to the announcement?" he asks.

"I didn't know there was an announcement. I was away that week." It's a horrendous excuse, and one that will no doubt reveal its flaws to them.

Without another word, he raises a knife and slashes it across my throat. My eyes widen in shock as I bleed out. I thought they would simply erase my memory. I didn't think they would *kill* me.

My last thought before the blackness descends is that at least I was able to write everything down. Someone will find it. I know it.

Chapter 15

Demonica

Years pass. More years than I can keep track of. My demons are satisfied, and we're essentially thriving. The thing most of them don't know is that we're running low on our slaves. We keep them alive as long as we can, and we breed them, but there aren't enough to sustain us. I don't know what to do about it.

We could maybe go longer between feedings, but I don't exactly know what that will do to us. We've all been feeding for so long on a specific schedule. I had everything planned out, and there was supposed to be enough for all of us indefinitely.

But years ago, we started noticing some infertility among the slaves. It could be a product of the environment we live in, it could be the feedings themselves. There's no way of knowing. Either way, I have to figure out a solution.

Then one day the solution presents itself to me in the form of a mermaid traveling into our realm. Her name is Elora Harbor. She tells me she's the grand mistress of Mermacovia. I almost kill her when she first emerges. Then I decide I should at least find out why she's here. Perhaps I can get something from her.

"Your Majesty," she addresses me, and I'm shocked, which

isn't easily accomplished. "I just discovered your story, and I had to find a way to come to you. I wish to pledge myself to you in any way I can. I'm here to serve the true queen, and I want to return you to your throne."

I still haven't said anything to her. I'm too stunned. But eventually, my brain starts working again. "You found my story?"

She nods vehemently. "Yes. It was written by someone named Crissa. She tells of how you're Surseiha's heir and that you were banished after being killed by the king. She also said that they erased everyone's memories from that time of you and your demons. The realm was in turmoil, and that was how they corrected the problem."

Crissa. I still haven't forgotten about her. It seems she did serve me properly in the end. The thought that I was erased from existence on Queridian should infuriate me, but I'm past that by this point. And why should I be upset when I have such a stupid and willing soul right in front of me who discovered my story? "And you're willing to do anything I need?"

"Yes, my queen."

"All right. I need you to smuggle me people."

"People, Your Majesty?"

Gods help me. This woman is not the brightest. But beggars can't be choosers.

"Yes. We were given slaves to feed off of when we were banished here, but are running dangerously low. I need you to bring me more. Otherwise we will all die."

Her eyes are wide, and I can tell that she's not thrilled with the prospect. She was no doubt going to offer me something useless.

"Let me make this easy for you, Elora Harbor. Either you

give me what I need, or I kill you right here and now in this godsforsaken land."

She pales and visibly swallows. "Of course I'll bring you as many people as I can, Your Majesty."

"Very good. You have one month."

I bring our palms together and do a quick spell over them, binding her to her word. She gasps at the magic that springs to life between us.

"You know how to do base magic?"

My brows furrow in confusion. Do people not know how to do it any longer?

"Yes. Do you not?"

"No, Your Majesty. The only ones who have the knowledge are the royals and some of the fae."

I growl. Of course the greedy fae would keep that knowledge for themselves. I mean, I would have done the same if I were Theon, but that's beside the point. I move on from that. I don't care what those half-wits are doing anymore.

"I've just bound you to me. You may not disobey me, and this will ensure your loyalty."

Terror lights her eyes, but she nods. I internally chuckle. Bitch didn't know what she was getting into when she came here.

"One month," I tell her again. "Now, go back home and get to work for me."

"Yes, Your Majesty." She bows and basically runs back to the portal.

One month later on the dot, she brings me seven people. Seven. One of each species. I thought there were only six species, but apparently a new one has made themselves known since I last lived there. Humans. I almost roll my eyes at the meager number. But I remind myself that it's better than nothing, and I now have someone working for me on the other side. She can continue to bring me more, and with the number of people she's taking, it won't arouse suspicion.

"Very good, Elora. Bring me more in another three months."

"Yes, Your Majesty."

And so it continues. Always seven. Never more than that. But it does the trick. It turns around our dire situation, and my demons are able to feed.

I always feed on the humans myself. Because they are so in tune with emotions, they always taste more exquisite to me. The human emotions give more substance for feeding, and they last longer. I don't tell any of the others that though. I want them all to myself.

Elora ages, and I know my luck won't last forever. It can be exhausting living so long, I think sometimes. But just when I'm sure she's not coming back, something else happens.

Another mermaid falls into my realm.

"Your Majesty, my mother told me about you. She wants me to continue to serve you. My name is Coralia."

I smile wickedly. My luck held.

Coralia proves to be ten times more capable and talented than her mother. She's exceedingly wicked, and she brings me many more cattle than her mother ever did, lacking a moral compass. She's perfect for my needs, and takes her own initiative. She recruits people on the ground running for me. One such helper is installed in the castle as a spy, and she's garnering support for me. Coralia is also giving Theon's descendant as much trouble as possible. I like her. Although, I can never admit as much to her. I need to keep her in line, and to do that I must be harsh.

There's not much she can do to bring me and my demons through, other than pushing for the races to mingle, but according to her, the royals have been consistent about keeping them apart. Which means the royal line still knows about me, even if no one else does. And they're worried I could come through. The thought brings a smile to my lips. I like the idea of Theon's precious line still having nightmares about me.

More and more people are brought through into my realm, and I relish in it. My demons and I feed more frequently than we ever have before, which means we're stronger than we've ever been. I have begun to share my human slaves with them to strengthen our power, and the emotions provide an abundance of nourishment that satisfies our need to feed. In the past, our slaves and cattle had become so despondent and full of despair that our race wasn't thriving. With all the new victims here, there is a refreshing influx of more pleasant emotions.

One day, I decide to head to the portal. I don't know what prompts me to do so. It hasn't been the normal length of time that I normally wait, but I'm drawn to it, like a moth to a flame.

I carry the stone in my hand, the sharp edges digging into my palm. I close my eyes and take a deep breath and attempt to walk into it. A swirling sensation builds within me. One I haven't felt in *thousands* of years. When I open my eyes again, I'm in a cave. I look around at the familiar space. I've been here before. I'm through. I'm finally back in Queridian.

Author Note

Thank you so much for reading *A Demon in the Dawn*! I really hope you enjoyed seeing this side of the villain in my Realm of Queridian series. I wanted to show the similarities between Ember and Demonica and demonstrate that Ember *could* have ended up like Demonica if she had made different choices.

The final installment in the Realm of Queridian series, *A Queen in the Ashes*, will *hopefully* be released on October 1.

If you enjoyed this book, please please please leave me a review. It is immensely helpful to us indie authors, and we need all the help we can get.

About the Author

L.J. Burkhart is a fantasy and romance author, as she loves all things paranormal and passionate. She has been a lifelong writer, starting with songs and poetry in the third grade, before eventually moving on to novels in her early twenties. When she isn't coming up with dramatic plot twists and steamy sex scenes, you can find her doing yoga, hanging out with her best bitches, baking, or reading, curled up on the couch with her husband and dog with a big glass of red wine.

You can connect with me on:

🌐 https://www.ljburkhart.com

Subscribe to my newsletter:

✉ http://eepurl.com/hRZzz5